Tim Burton's NIGHTMARE BEFORE CHRISTMAS

A ROUNDTABLE PRESS BOOK

THE FILM
THE ART ⊙ THE VISION

TIM BURTON'S
NIGHTMARE
BEFORE
CHRISTMAS

FRANK THOMPSON

FOREWORD BY TIM BURTON

WITH THE COMPLETE LYRICS
FROM THE FILM

HYPERION

NEW YORK

Frank Thompson is the author of *Alamo Movies, William A. Wellman, Between Action and Cut: Five American Directors,* and several other books, as well as articles in such publications as *American Film, Film Comment,* the *Boston Globe,* the *Houston Chronicle,* and the *San Francisco Chronicle.* He has also written scripts for *Hollywood Babylon* and other television programs.

A ROUNDTABLE PRESS BOOK
Directors: Susan E. Meyer, Marsha Melnick
Project Editor: Sue Heinemann
Interior Design: Michaelis/Carpelis Design Inc.
Assistant Editor: Ross Horowitz
Principal Photographer: Elizabeth J. Annas
Hyperion Project Editor: Mary Ann Naples
Project Editor for Tim Burton Productions: Jill Jacobs

Library of Congress Cataloging-in-Publication Data
Thompson, Frank T.
Tim Burton's nightmare before Christmas: the film, the art, the vision / by Frank Thompson : foreword by Tim Burton.—1st ed.
        p. cm.
Includes index.
ISBN 0-7868-8066-X
1. Nightmare before Christmas (Motion picture) I. Title
PN1997.N522353T5 1993
791.43'72—dc20   93-8736
                                                                      CIP

First Paperback Edition
10 9 8 7 6 5 4 3 2 1

For Claire, always

Table of Contents

FOREWORD

Nightmare Before Christmas is a movie I've wanted to make for over a decade, since I worked as an animator at Walt Disney Studios in the early eighties. It started as a poem I wrote, influenced by the style of my favorite children's author, Dr. Seuss. I made several drawings of the characters and the settings and began planning it as a film.

I thought at first that *Nightmare Before Christmas* would make a good holiday special for television, although I also considered other forms, including a children's book. At the time, I think, it was too weird for Disney. I moved on to other things, but I never forgot it.

Although the title makes the film sound a little scary, I see *Nightmare Before Christmas* as a positive story, without any truly bad characters. The characters are trying to do something good and just get a little mixed up.

Like a lot of people, I grew up loving the animated specials like *Rudolph the Red-Nosed Reindeer* and *How the Grinch Stole Christmas* that appeared on TV every year. I wanted to create something with the same kind of feeling and warmth.

Tim Burton first sketched Jack Skellington, the movie's hero, in his notebook (opposite, top), over ten years ago, while he was making his short film Vincent at Disney Studios. He later drew most of the other characters in Nightmare—including the Mayor (below) and Sally (opposite, bottom), shown in preliminary versions here.

Nightmare is the story of Jack Skellington, the Pumpkin King of Halloweenland, who discovers Christmas and immediately wants to celebrate this strange holiday himself. I love Jack. He has a lot of passion and energy; he's always looking for a feeling. That's what he finds in Christmas Town. He is a bit misguided and his emotions take over, but he gets everybody excited. The setting may be odd and a little unsettling, but there are no real villains in the film. It's a celebration of Halloween and Christmas—my two favorite holidays.

I decided early on that I wanted to tell this story through stop-motion animation. I have always loved this medium, but it is challenging. One danger is that the audience may become overwhelmed by the technique and get distracted from the emotion.

Luckily, I was able to entrust *Nightmare Before Christmas* to my friend Henry Selick, the most brilliant stop-motion director around. We have a similar sensibility, and he was able to take my original drawings and bring them to life. He gathered together an amazing crew in San Francisco—a wonderful group of artists, all working toward the same vision. Everybody put their heart into it—Henry, the composer Danny Elfman, the screenwriter Caroline Thompson, the animators,

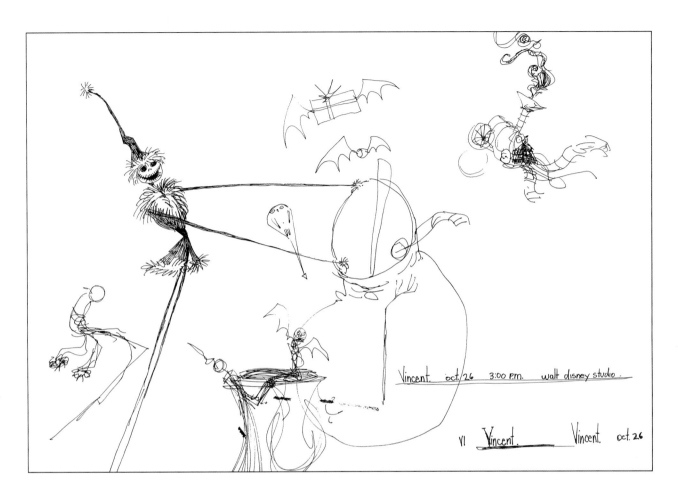

Vincent. oct/26 3:00 P.M. walt disney studio.

VI Vincent. Vincent. oct. 26

everybody down the line—making it an incredibly challenging, and rewarding experience.

Nightmare Before Christmas is deeper in my heart than any other film. It is more beautiful than I imagined it would be, thanks to Henry and his talented crew of artists, animators, and designers. As I watch it, I know I will never have this feeling again. *Nightmare Before Christmas* is special. It is a film that I have always known I had to make. More important, it is a film I have always wanted to see. Now I can. It has been worth the wait. I think there are few projects like that in your life.

Tim Burton

Jack Skellington has many sides to his personality, expressing a range of emotions, as Tim Burton's sketches (above) show. Early in the movie Jack wanders alone through the cemetery in Halloweenland (above right), singing a melancholy song.

INTRODUCTION

In every Tim Burton film there are a few elements you can count on. The script offers an eccentric, funny, and exciting mixture of goofiness and morbidity. The sets and costumes are heavily influenced by German Expressionism and the Universal horror films Burton loves so. The lead character is an outsider—"a loner . . . a rebel," as Pee-wee calls himself in *Pee-wee's Big Adventure* (1985)—someone who longs for a place in society that he can never fully occupy. And through the entire enterprise runs a healthy and audacious dose of irony.

In the case of *Tim Burton's Nightmare Before Christmas*, the irony exists off screen as well as on. The movie is based on a poem that Burton wrote and illustrated over a decade ago, while he was working as an animator at Walt Disney Studios. Although at the time the Disney Company rejected the idea, today it is the film's enthusiastic producer.

Burton actually met the film's director Henry Selick at Disney Studios, where Selick was also an animator. Both were disillusioned with the work there and impatient with animating "cute little foxes." Now, they have joined forces to make an animated film for Disney in which there isn't a cute fox in sight. In fact, there isn't anything cute about *Nightmare Before Christmas*. It's just funny, a little scary, and unrelentingly creative.

In his early years at Disney, Burton "did not fit into the track of the average animator," notes Denise Di Novi, one of *Nightmare*'s producers.

She explains that Disney "saw very quickly that he was very creative and had unusual ideas." Yet when he left the studio, his ideas just went in a file somewhere.

Burton went on to become the director of such successful feature films as *Batman* (1989) and *Edward Scissorhands* (1990). But he retained his fondness for animation. And he kept his pet project—his poem "The Nightmare Before Christmas"—in mind.

From the start Burton wanted to produce *Nightmare Before Christmas* in stop-motion animation, a form that has never enjoyed wide popularity in the United States. "I love stop-motion," Burton exclaims. "There's always a certain beauty to it, yet it's unusual at the same time. It has reality. Especially on a project like *Nightmare,* where the characters are so unreal, it makes them more believable, more solid."

Burton admits that stop-motion is a challenging medium and points out that before doing *Nightmare,* "I'd never seen a stop-motion film that completely worked for me." But he was always convinced that stop-motion was perfect for his story about Jack Skellington and his misguided attempt to take over Christmas.

When Burton eventually decided to return to his pet project, he realized two things: Disney was the only studio successfully producing animated films, and because Burton came up with *Nightmare* while he was working at Disney, the studio owned it. Disney had, in the meantime, undergone a change in regime. Under Michael Eisner and Jeffrey Katzenberg, the studio had made a new commitment to animation—a drive that produced *The Little Mermaid* (1989), *Beauty and the Beast* (1991), and *Aladdin* (1992).

Taking a second look at Burton's original proposal, Katzenberg was immediately enthusiastic. "This is unlike any movie ever made before," Katzenberg says. "It is a pioneering film effort that is very much part of Walt Disney's film heritage." At the same time Katzenberg describes it as "a movie with a big heart and a lot of emotion."

Even though *Nightmare* was Burton's pet project, he decided not to direct it himself, feeling that it could be properly brought to life only by a master of stop-motion animation. He chose Henry

Halloweenland is full of jagged, pointed shapes. The drawing below shows an early version of the view just outside the gate of Jack's house.

Selick, who had produced several acclaimed short films and done some stunning work for MTV.

"Working with Tim Burton has been a wonderful collaboration," remarks Selick. "He cares deeply about the film, but has left me enormous freedom to make the film work. The film looks like his hand is in it everywhere—that's part of my job."

Although Burton, Danny Elfman (who wrote the songs that tell the story), and Rick Heinrichs (who, as visual consultant, helped develop the look of the film) were all based in Los Angeles, Selick was located in San Francisco—as were many of the stop-motion and special-effects artists who were best qualified to tackle this unprecedented production. San Francisco Studios, a huge warehouse, became the home of Skellington Productions, named after *Nightmare*'s lead character, Jack Skellington.

The first item on the agenda was to shoot some test footage to prove to Disney—and everybody involved—that the movie could be made. "We built a couple of puppets," says Selick, "recorded some temporary dialogue, and produced a little scene." Although it was only about twenty seconds of film, in stop-motion animation that is a considerable amount of work.

A core group of artists began to form at Skellington Productions, including director of photography Pete Kozachik, supervising animator Eric Leighton, storyboard artist Joe Ranft, and mold-making supervisor John Reed. "We worked a lot of very long days," explains Reed. "We talked constantly to each other and tried to solve all the problems that we could

After walking for hours through the forest, Jack discovers four trees with unusual doors (shown below right in a sketch based on a Tim Burton drawing). He opens one door— and falls down into Christmas Town (below).

anticipate. While you don't want to have too many cooks spoiling the broth, you do want to hear what different people have to say."

After Disney approved the test and gave Burton and Selick the go-ahead, they began building a giant stop-motion crew from the ground up. "It was a great opportunity," notes Selick, "to bring together the best mold makers, sculptors, armature makers, fabricators, set builders, camera people, computer people, and—at the top of the heap—animators with a very rare approach to animation."

Denise Di Novi stresses how unusual putting together such a large production unit was. "Usually you do stop-motion for a one-minute commercial," she comments. "But we needed to build a whole studio from scratch. And we had to comb the world for animators."

The careful search for the best in the field paid off. As John Reed says, "We became a team, with everybody working toward the same end." Selick's own expertise as an animator was particularly important, according to Reed, in such a large-scale production. "He knew the terrain."

Without question, *Tim Burton's Nightmare Before Christmas* is the most complex and elaborate stop-motion animated film ever made. But although Selick and his crew at times took advantage of high-tech tools, such as computers and video, the underlying technique was as basic and low-tech as you can get. Selick comments, "Many people would say that what we're doing is obsolete, that computers are completely taking over animation. But *Nightmare Before Christmas* should change some minds. I hope this film will make people consider stop-motion as something wildly new."

The key to stop-motion animation is this: moving pictures don't move. Today, normal 35mm film runs through a projector at twenty-four frames per second. Each frame consists of a single photograph. When the frames are projected and speed past the eye, the rapid succession of still images suggests movement that really isn't there.

Stop-motion animation is based on that illusion. Take a puppet or prop or some other object, pose it and photograph it with a single frame of movie film. Move it slightly and then snap another frame. Do this twenty-four times and you have a single second of motion picture footage. Do that several hundred thousand more times, and you have a feature-length stop-motion movie like *Nightmare Before Christmas*.

How does this relate to traditional animation? Most animated films—including such Disney classics as *Snow White and the Seven Dwarfs* (1937) and *Fantasia* (1940)—are produced by painting pictures

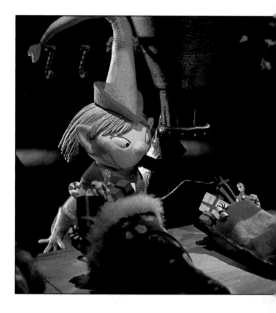

In Christmas Town, Santa's elves are seen busily making toys and stuffing stockings. A similar activity takes place in Halloween Town, but with a twist.

A jaunty Jack returns to Halloween Town in a snowmobile stuffed with Christmas wares.

on clear sheets of celluloid, which are then laid over painted backgrounds. This method is called "cel animation." Both cel and stop-motion animation—when done right—create a separate image for each frame, and there are many similarities in the way the films are produced. But there is a major difference. Cel animation is essentially a two-dimensional art, while stop-motion animation uses three-dimensional "characters" that have a tangible physical presence. The figures are not drawn but built. And they do actually move (when an animator raises the puppet's leg or twists its arm).

Because it looks so different from traditional cel animation, *Tim Burton's Nightmare Before Christmas* may appear to have been produced using a "new" technique. However, stop-motion animation has been around nearly as long as motion pictures have existed. It even predates conventional cel animation. No one is quite sure who made the first stop-motion animated film, but whoever it was saw the connection between the way film works and the way to make inanimate objects appear to come alive on screen.

In the early days of the cinema, motion picture cameras were operated with a hand crank. One complete turn of the crank exposed one frame of film. When shooting live action, the cameraperson simply kept a steady rhythm. The film, projected at the same speed, gave the illusion of natural motion. Films in the early twentieth century were usually shot at a rate of sixteen to twenty frames per second.

The first step toward animation was the discovery that if you stopped the camera, replaced the person or object being filmed with a different person or object, and started the camera again, a magical transformation took place. In 1895 the Edison Company illustrated this theory in a particularly grisly way. In a film called *The Execution of Mary, Queen of Scots,* the actress who played Mary was marched to the chopping block. When the executioner raised his ax, the camera was stopped and the actress was replaced by a dummy. Filming resumed, the ax fell, and a head tumbled. Audiences did not detect the trickery since Mary's approach to the chopping block and her beheading seemed to be a continuous series of actions.

Once this secret got out, dozens of early filmmakers started producing "trick films"—cinematic versions of magic shows in which both people and objects were moved or transformed without the use of wires or mirrors. These works were not, at first, truly stop-motion films, but simply a way to make the impossible appear to happen.

In 1898 film pioneer J. Stuart Blackton and his partner Albert E. Smith were shooting a trick film on a New York rooftop. As they started and stopped the camera to make the substitutions, clouds of steam from the building's electrical generator drifted across the background. When they projected the film, they noticed that the clouds seemed to hop around the screen.

Smith later wrote, "These unplanned adventures with puffs of steam led us to some weird effects. In *A Visit to the Spiritualist* wall pictures, chairs and tables flew in and out, and characters disappeared willy-nilly—done by stopping the camera, making changes, and starting again."

*E*very character and object in the film evolved through sketches and color studies like these before being molded and painted in final, three-dimensional form. The saw below has been turned upside down from its position in the film to do its job here.

The real motion of the film takes place in between each frame as the animators slightly shift the puppets' positions. In a crowd scene like this one in Halloween Town, the animators may have to adjust twenty or more puppets before each take. Sally (shown below in a colored-in version of one of Tim Burton's black-and-white sketches) brings romance to Halloween Town.

In 1898 Smith and Blackton produced what they claimed was the very first stop-motion film in the United States, *The Humpty Dumpty Circus*. As Smith described it, "I used my little daughter's set of wooden circus performers and animals, whose movable joints enabled us to place them in balanced positions. It was a tedious process in as much as the movement could be achieved only by photographing separately each change of position. I suggested we obtain a patent on the process. Blackton felt it wasn't important enough. However, others quickly borrowed the technique, improving upon it greatly."

Unfortunately *The Humpty Dumpty Circus* seems to have vanished—as have more than half the movies produced before 1950. But within a few years, stop-motion experiments were plentiful. The Russian animator Ladislas Starevich, for example, created some breathtaking (and oddly disturbing) stop-motion films in which he animated puppets of bugs, frogs, and other creatures.

Other masters of stop-motion through the years include Willis O'Brien, the brilliant animator who gave life to King Kong in 1933, and O'Brien's protégé Ray Harryhausen, who created dazzling special effects for such fantasy classics as *The Beast from 20,000 Fathoms* (1953), *The Seventh Voyage of Sinbad* (1958), and *Jason and the Argonauts* (1963).

George Pal was yet another stop-motion whiz. His "Puppetoons" of the thirties and forties are direct ancestors of *Tim Burton's Nightmare Before Christmas*. Pal carved his puppets from wood and gave them different facial expressions and lip movements by using dozens of replacement heads for each puppet. This same technique, refined in plastic instead of wood, allows *Nightmare*'s "stars," Jack Skellington and Sally, to talk, smile, and sing.

In the seventies and eighties, stop-motion began to come into its own. The technique has been most frequently used as a special-effects tool by companies such as Industrial Light and Magic for science fiction epics like *Star Wars* (1977), *The Terminator* (1984), and *Robocop* (1987). When you see a robot doing something particularly impossible in a movie scene, chances are it is a miniature figure that was animated frame by meticulous frame.

At the same time, though, many animators have been exploring the artistic potential of stop-motion as an end in itself. Will Vinton made "Claymation"—animation using clay figures—a household word with his highly popular California Raisins. Vinton also produced a feature-length Claymation film, *The Adventures of Mark Twain* (1985)—a brave, but unsuccessful, experiment.

Paul Reubens's wildly imaginative Saturday morning show *Pee-wee's Playhouse* (1987–90) became a showcase for innovative stop-motion work from companies such as England's Aardman Animations and New York's Broadcast Arts, as well as clay animators Dave Daniels, Tom Gasek, Craig Bartlett, and many others. Aardman Animations produced the original "Penny" cartoons for *Pee-wee's Playhouse* and the remarkable "Sledgehammer" video for singer Peter Gabriel. One of Aardman's clay-animated shorts, *Creature Comforts,* won an Academy Award as Best

When Jack decides to take over Christmas, he sends Lock, Shock, and Barrel on a delicate mission—to kidnap "Sandy Claws." The three impish trick-or-treaters scheme with glee (left). The characters themselves evolved out of Tim Burton's drawings, like the one of Lock below.

Animated Short Film in 1990. The rise of MTV and the increasing popularity of stop-motion as an advertising tool brought work to such prominent animation houses as Olive Jar Studio, John Lemmon Films, Sculptoons, Colossal Pictures, and Cosgrove Hall.

Many of the artists and animators who worked on *Tim Burton's Nightmare Before Christmas* gained experience with these companies. But one little-seen television series from 1988 probably had a more direct impact on *Nightmare* than anything else. Art Clokey, the creator of Gumby and Pokey, the little clay boy and horse of the 1950s, decided to resurrect his characters for a new generation. The result was *The New Gumby,* ninety-nine episodes of which were produced in San Francisco at Clokey's Premavision Studio.

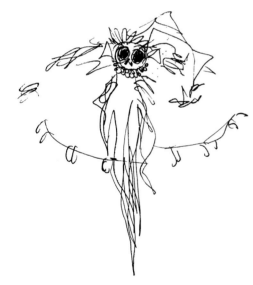

Jack's delight in playing Santa is translated from Tim Burton's initial sketch (below) to another artist's drawing (bottom).

The original *Gumby* introduced an entire generation to low-tech stop-motion. The eighties remake created a new wave of stop-motion artists. Several of the *Nightmare* animators learned the ropes on this low-budget show.

"It was an amazing experience," claims animator Angie Glocka. "You learned while you were on television. When I started there, I had exactly one four-day-weekend's worth of experience as a stop-motion animator. But they needed people, so I got a chance to learn almost everything a stop-motion animator should know."

Animator Mike Belzer also received valuable training on *The New Gumby.* "The process was similar to *Nightmare,*" he explains, "except that what we did as run-throughs on this show were final shots on *Gumby.* The production schedule was fierce; we had a certain quota per week, which is very different from *Nightmare.* On *Gumby,* it might not look great, but it was good enough to go on TV. Here, they told us, 'Do your best; make it perfect.'"

Stop-motion has a long and fascinating history, and some great stop-motion animators have produced brilliant work. But everyone involved behind-the-scenes with *Nightmare Before Christmas* agrees: no

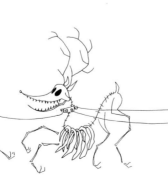

Poor Jack—it doesn't work out as he had planned. He's shot down out of the sky and ends up in a Real World cemetery (shown at left in the final rendering, on which the shot is based). He has to hurry to rescue Santa from Oogie Boogie, a nightmarish creature who lives up to his name. Oogie's lair is full of torture devices (shown below in one of many concept drawings done to figure out how to make the evil machines work).

one has ever done anything as complex and meticulous and ambitious as this feature-length film.

Animator Paul Berry, who worked with England's stop-motion studio Cosgrove Hall before coming to California to work on *Nightmare,* says, "Everything about this has been completely different from what I was used to. I was used to setting up a shot, animating it, then going on to work on the next; you might do two or three shots in a day. Here, a lot of time was spent on getting each shot to look great, not only compositionally but also on the level of acting. The amount of energy poured into each shot was unusual. I'd never worked on anything like this before."

In the end *Tim Burton's Nightmare Before Christmas* looks nothing like Disney's previous animated films. "It's a very different kind of movie for Disney," emphasizes Denise Di Novi. "It's more sophisticated and darker, more eccentric, than the studio's other animated movies." Yet Di Novi believes that the Disney Company is excited about broadening its base. "This is an opportunity for Disney to break out of the mold a little and surprise people."

"I think the film's breathtaking," exclaims Jeffrey Katzenberg. "Audiences walking into a movie theater will have their socks knocked off. It's indescribable. No matter what you think the movie is going to be, you'll be surprised. There's nothing more rewarding for a studio to be able to do than to surprise and captivate movie audiences. *Nightmare Before Christmas* is a visual treat. It has great heart and soul."

DID YOU EVER WONDER WHERE HOLIDAYS COME FROM? IF YOU THINK THEY JUST APPEAR OUT OF THIN AIR EVERY YEAR, THEN YOU OBVIOUSLY DON'T KNOW ABOUT THE HOLIDAY WORLDS. EACH WORLD SPENDS A WHOLE YEAR PLANNING ITS SPECIAL DAY. DID YOU THINK ALL THOSE COLORFUL EASTER EGGS JUST ARRIVED BY MAGIC? NOT AT ALL. IT TAKES A LOT OF TIME AND HARD WORK. TODAY, THE CITIZENS OF HALLOWEENLAND ARE CELEBRATING THEIR DAY, THE MOST TERRIFYING DAY OF THE YEAR.

The Little Witch (shown in a color study here) and her companion (shown on page 15) zoom through the sky on their broomsticks, singing about Halloween.

THIS IS HALLOWEEN

SHADOW
> *Boys and Girls of every age*
> *Wouldn't you like to see something strange?*

SIAMESE SHADOW
> *Come with us and you will see . . .*
> *This our town of Halloween!*

PUMPKIN PATCH CHORUS
> *This is Halloween, this is Halloween!*
> *Pumpkins scream in the dead of night—*

GHOSTS
> *This is Halloween, everybody make a scene*
> *Trick or treat 'til the neighbors gonna die of fright*
> *It's our town. Everybody scream*
> *In this town of Halloween . . .*

CREATURE UNDER BED
> *I am the one hiding under your bed,*
> *Teeth ground sharp and eyes glowing red.*

MAN UNDER THE STAIRS
> *I am the one hiding under your stairs*
> *Fingers like snakes and spiders in my hair.*

CORPSE CHORUS
> *This is Halloween, this is Halloween,*

VAMPIRES 1, 2, 3, 4 (separately)
> *Halloween . . .*
> *Halloween . . .*
> *Halloween . . .*
> *Halloween . . .*

VAMPIRES (little, squeaky and high voices)
> *In this town, we call home,*
> *Everyone hail to the Pumpkin Song!*

MAYOR
> *In this town, don't we love it now* [optimistic]
> *Everybody's waiting for the next surprise* [pessimistic].

CORPSE CHORUS
> *'Round that corner, man, Hiding in a trashcan*
> *Something's waiting now to pounce and*
>   *how you'll—*

HARLEQUIN DEMON, WEREWOLF,
AND MELTING MAN
> *—Scream! This is Halloween,*
> *Red 'n black, slimy green . . .*

The Vampire's tiny, insectlike head is framed in blood-red above its huge black body in the final color design above. The graphic look of Halloweenland in sketches like the one below is carried through to the final set.

When the Clown tears off his happy face—there's nothing there. The sketches below him show some of the early ideas for buildings in Halloweenland.

WEREWOLF

> *Aren't you scared?*

WITCHES

> *Well, that's just fine!*
> *Say it once, say it twice,*
> *Take the chance and roll the dice*
> *Ride with the moon in the dead of night (oh)*

HANGING TREE

> *Everybody scream, everybody scream*

HANGED MEN

> *In our town of Halloween.*

CLOWN WITH TEARAWAY FACE

> *I am the guy with the tearaway face . . .*
> *Here in a flash and gone without a trace.*

GHOUL

> *I am the one who when you call—Who's there?*
> *I am the wind blowing through your hair.*

OOGIE BOOGIE (SHADOW)

> *I am the shadow on the moon at night,*
> *Filling your dreams to the brim with fright.*

A preliminary design for the hanging tree (left) suggests its full, deep voice, in contrast to the high, thin chorus of the hanged men. The werewolf's gleaming green eyes add to his sinister look in the final color design (below). Seen together, there is no question that the characters on the set (below left) belong to Halloween.

The eerie landscape of Halloweenland rises behind the drinking well in the Town Square (above). The Corpse Child (below) always has his eyes sewn shut.

CORPSE CHORUS
> *This is Halloween, This is Halloween*
> *Halloween Halloween! Halloween Halloween!*

CHILD CORPSE TRIO
> *Tender Lumplings everywhere*
> *Life's no fun without a good scare.*

PARENT CORPSES
> *That's our job, but we're not mean*
> *In our town of Halloween.*

CORPSE CHORUS
> *In this town—*

MAYOR (optimistic)
> *—don't we love it now?*

MAYOR WITH CORPSE CHORUS
Everyone's waiting for the next surprise.

CORPSE CHORUS
Skeleton Jack might catch you in the back and
Scream like a banshee make you jump
    out of your SKIN!
This is Halloween, everyone scream

SALLY
Won't ya please make way for a special guy . . .

CORPSE CHORUS
Our man Jack is King of the Pumpkin Patch.
Everyone hail to the Pumpkin King now.

EVERYONE
This is Halloween, THIS IS HALLOWEEN
Halloween Halloween Halloween Halloween

CORPSE CHILD TRIO
In this place we call home
Everyone hail to the Pumpkin Song.

The scarecrow Pumpkin King (above) is pulled through the streets before he sets himself on fire and leaps into the fountain— to rematerialize as the gentlemanly Jack Skellington. After the celebration is over, Jack slowly walks away, tossing a coin to some street musicians (left).

Jack's house (shown in the final design opposite) has a tall, spindly tower with a study on top—a fitting den for the almost impossibly thin puppet (opposite, top right).

Jack Skellington, the Pumpkin King of Halloweenland, is "tall and thin with a bat bow tie." He has a face like a skeleton and a genius for terror. But, at heart, Jack Skellington is a gentle, melancholy guy, tired of his crown and mournfully singing, "He would give it all up if he only could." He wants to do something more than scare people with his blood-curdling scream.

"His melancholy comes from his loneliness and isolation," notes screenwriter Caroline Thompson, "from his feelings of 'been here, done that.' He's one of those people where everything seems to be going great on the outside but underneath he's pretty miserable."

In Tim Burton's view, "Jack is basically trying to do good, but he's misperceived." When Jack takes on the role of Santa, Burton explains, "he thinks everything is wonderful, but he's actually driving the whole world into a state of panic. There's something very beautiful and sad and funny about that."

Jack Skellington has many different facets to his personality. When we first see him on the screen, before we know his importance to the story, it's Halloween, and Jack is dressed like a scarecrow with a large pumpkin head. He seems stiff and clumsy until he jumps into the fountain and reemerges, making his grand entrance as himself—quite debonair in his black-and-white striped suit with tails.

Throughout the film Jack shows us other aspects of his personality: he is depressed about the emptiness in his soul as he wanders through the forest, but then overcome with delight when he falls into the sparkling Christmas Town. He is a demonic little boy when he dresses up as Santa Claus and delivers ghoulish presents from his coffin sleigh and an avenging angel when he later roars into action to rescue Santa and set things right.

At first director Henry Selick thought that, with his skeletal frame, Jack would be impossible to design and ani-

NIGHTMARE BEFORE CHRISTMAS

mate. But he admits that Jack "ended up looking incredibly dapper, just as Tim intended, and he also moves elegantly."

"There's a very definite style to the way Jack walks," adds animator Paul Berry. "It defines what his whole personality is about. He's this regal figure." Berry stresses the emotional quality of Jack's every movement. "When you animate Jack from the outside you have to deal with what's inside him as well."

29

JACK ACCEPTS THE APPLAUSE OF HIS ADORING PUBLIC. THE MAYOR SAYS THAT THIS YEAR'S HALLOWEEN WAS THE MOST HORRIBLE EVER. JACK SHOULD BE PROUD AND HAPPY. BUT ONLY ONE PERSON IN THE CROWD— A SEWN-TOGETHER RAG DOLL OF A GIRL NAMED SALLY—SEES THAT JACK REACTS TO THE PRAISE WITH MELANCHOLY. AS JACK WALKS AWAY, TO BE BY HIMSELF, SALLY FOLLOWS AT A DISTANCE, LISTENING TO HIS LAMENT.

JACK'S LAMENT

Jack sings his lament in the Halloweenland cemetery (below), dancing on the grave-stones and crypts, which are decorated with gargoyles like the one opposite (top). At one point he even takes off his head "to recite Shakespearean quotations" (storyboard, opposite bottom).

JACK

> There are few who'd deny, at what I do I am the best
>> For my talents are renowned far and wide
> When it comes to surprises in the moonlit night,
>> I excel without ever even trying.
>
> With the slightest little effort of my ghostlike charms
>> I have seen grown men give out a shriek
> With the wave of my hand, and a well-placed moan,
>> I have swept the very bravest off their feet.

Yet year after year, it's the same routine
And I grow so weary of the sound of screams
And I, Jack, the PUMPKIN KING!
Have grown so tired of the same old thing . . .

Oh, somewhere deep inside of these bones
An emptiness began to grow
There's something out there far from my home
A longing that I've never known
. . . I've never known.

I'm a master of fright, and a demon of light
And I'll scare you right out of your pants, boy
To a guy in Kentucky, I'm Mister Unlucky
And I'm known throughout England and France, boy

And since I am dead, I can take off my head
To recite Shakespearean quotations
No animal or man can scream like I can
With the fury of my recitations.

But who here would ever understand
That the Pumpkin King with the skeleton grin
Would tire of his crown—if they only understood
He would give it all up if he only could
. . . if he only could

Oh, there's an empty place in my bones
That calls out for something unknown
The fame and praise, come year after year,
Does nothing for these empty tears
. . . these empty tears . . .

The Zero puppet (below) becomes transparent on the screen (right).

Jack Skellington's little dog Zero is the perfect Halloweenland pet. He's both faithful and playful—and he's a ghost with an illuminated pumpkin nose who floats just above the ground.

Like most dogs, Zero sleeps most of the day, sometimes in a little basket in Jack's room and sometimes in his doghouse in the cemetery. But when Jack goes for a walk, he's ready to follow, and he likes to play catch with Jack's ribs.

Zero doesn't always understand Jack's strange actions, but he's always ready to lend a helping paw. On the foggy Christmas Eve, when it looks as if Jack's plans are about to be shattered, a bril-

liant light cuts through the night. Jack realizes at once that Zero, with his shining nose, is the one to guide his sleigh.

As Jack laments his fate (left), Sally hides behind the tombstones, listening in sympathy (below). She knows how he feels, but she is afraid to speak.

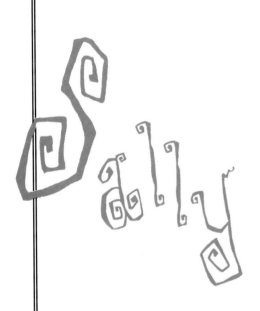

Sally concocts a variety of brews in her kitchen in the Evil Scientist's lab (above right). In her room, by her window or on her bed, she thinks about Jack (opposite).

In a more conventional film, with a more conventional heroine, Sally might be little more than Jack Skellington's romantic interest. But in *Nightmare* she becomes Jack's kindred spirit, the only one who can truly understand how he feels.

Sally is essentially an animated rag doll. As John Reed, mold-making supervisor, puts it, "She's basically a Frankenstein-like puppet. She looks like she's sewn together from a bunch of scraps." Her balance is precarious. Her arms flop. Her mouth is a tragic slash.

Sally is certainly a far cry from conventional ideals of beauty. But she doesn't even raise an eyebrow in Halloweenland, where everybody looks a little . . . different.

"The Sally character came from something real deep in me," confesses Tim Burton, "a sort of weird impulse. She came out of drawings with this strange stitching image that I'd been thinking about for a while." He laughs, "I guess I work out a lot of psychological problems with these things."

"My first inclination was to make Sally a sort of little match girl, a will-o'-the-wisp," says Caroline Thompson. "But she seemed far too passive; there was no juice to her." At that early point, composer Danny Elfman had not yet written "Sally's Song," and, Thompson had to struggle to find a more arresting personality for Sally.

It wasn't until she looked at some early test footage that

Thompson found her solution. As she describes it, "When I saw the way they animated her, that she moved like a spider, I was inspired to strengthen her character."

In the movie Sally is the creation of Dr. Finklestein, the Evil Scientist. Although he didn't do such a great job in finding matching parts when he built her, he at least—even if inadvertently—gave Sally more than the recommended daily requirement of spunk.

The Evil Scientist also gave each of Sally's limbs a life of its own. She can remove any part of her body, and it will remain active on its own— which can be very helpful.

When, for example, Dr. Finklestein attempts to restrain Sally by holding onto her arm, she simply unstitches it and runs away, leaving the arm behind to pummel the scientist on the head. While trying to rescue Santa Claus from the terrible tortures that the monstrous Oogie Boogie has in mind, Sally quickly detaches her hands, which clamber off to untie Santa's bonds.

"I love the idea that when she jumps out a window," says Thompson, "she can sew herself back together again."

Thompson stresses that Sally "is Jack's truest friend, resourceful and brave. Only she understands what Jack is going through because she, too, dreams of something else from life. They are very much alike, but there is one crucial difference: while Jack's dilemma gives *Nightmare Before Christmas* its plot, Sally's gives it its heart."

The Christmas tree door twinkles with goodies, and when Jack opens it for a peek, it literally pulls him in—to another world. He lands, startled, on a mound of snow, wondering "What's this?" (below).

JACK WANDERS FARTHER AND FARTHER INTO THE WOODS, FEELING ALL ALONE—EXCEPT FOR HIS FAITHFUL GHOST DOG ZERO. BY AND BY HE COMES TO AN UNUSUAL FOREST, WHERE EACH TREE HAS A COLORFUL DOORWAY. ONE DOOR IS SHAPED LIKE AN EASTER EGG; ANOTHER LIKE A VALENTINE. JACK IS ATTRACTED TO THE BEAUTIFUL DOOR SHAPED LIKE A CHRISTMAS TREE. HE OPENS IT . . . AND FALLS AND FALLS THROUGH A TUNNEL OF SWIRLING SNOW, LANDING WITH A THUMP. THEN HE SITS UP AND LOOKS AROUND.

WHAT'S THIS?

JACK

> What's this? What's this?
> There's color everywhere . . . What's this?
> There're white things in the air . . . What's this?
> I can't believe my eyes I must be dreaming,
> Wake up, Jack, this isn't fair . . . What's this?
>
> What's this? What's this?
> There's something very wrong . . . What's this?
> There're people singing songs . . . What's this?
>
> The streets are lined with
> Little creatures laughing,
> Everybody seems so happy,
> Have I possibly gone daffy . . . ?
> What is this . . . ? What's this?

Jack first sees the view of Christmas Town at left, with Santa's factory gleaming in back. Entranced, he tumbles down the hill into a world of colorful gingerbread buildings like those in the bottom drawing. He's never seen toys like the one in the design below.

The sketches of objects in Christmas Town, from the brightly colored train above to the playful, rounded merry-go-round figures opposite, are totally different from those for Halloweenland. In a drawing of the interior of the elves' home (right), Jack glimpses a pet penguin snoozing by the fire.

There're children throwing snowballs
Here instead of throwing heads.
They're busy building toys
And absolutely no one's dead.

There's frost on every window,
Oh, I can't believe my eyes,
And in my bones I feel a warmth
That's coming from inside . . .

Oh, look, what's this?

They're hanging mistletoe . . . They kiss—
Why that looks so unique . . . Inspired!
They're gathering around to hear a story,
Roasting chestnuts on a fire . . . What's this?

What's this? In here
They've got a little tree . . . how queer!
And who would ever think . . . and why?

They're covering it with
Tiny little things, they've got
Electric lights on strings, and there's a
Smile on everyone, so now
Correct me if I'm wrong . . .
This looks like fun,
This looks like fun,
Oh, could it be I got my wish . . . ? What's this?

Every object in Christmas Town was drawn and then built, from the candy-cane ladders in this shot to the engine opposite. Often, as with the preliminary design for Santa's sled below, the drawings went through revisions. And there might be later changes, as the object was being built.

Oh my, what now?
The children are asleep . . . But look—
There's nothing underneath . . . No ghouls
No witches here to scream and scare them
            . . . or ensnare them . . .

Only cozy little things
Secure inside their dreamland . . . What's this?

The monsters are all missing
And the nightmares can't be found
And in their place there seems to be
Good feeling all around . . .

Instead of screams I swear I can hear
Music in the air.
The smell of cakes and pies
Is absolutely everywhere . . .

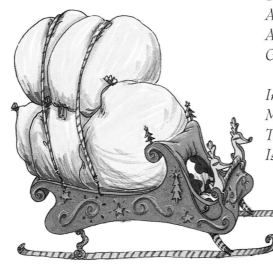

The sights, the sounds,
They're everywhere and all around . . .
I've never felt so good before . . .
The empty place inside of me is filling up
I simply cannot get enough.

I want it, oh, I want it . . .
Oh, I want it for my own.
I've got to know
I've got to know
What is this place that I have found?

WHAT IS THIS???

Santa Claus

When Jack Skellington has his first entrancing look at Christmas Town, there is one figure who fascinates him more than any other. But he mishears his name. Because he doesn't know any better—and since it sounds more natural to his Halloween ears—Jack calls this wonderful person "Sandy Claws." The first time the two meet, Jack is surprised: "Why, you have hands! You don't have claws at all!"

Armature maker Blair Clark describes *Nightmare*'s Santa as "a big, fat, round guy with little spindly legs. He has a lot of facial expression, as Oogie does. But Santa needs a more human, recognizable face. And he has to move right. If he doesn't, the audience will know."

Santa opens his door—to trouble.

IN HALLOWEENLAND EVERYONE IS WORRIED ABOUT JACK, WHO HAS
BEEN GONE ALL NIGHT. SALLY HEARS THE ALARMS WAIL, BUT SHE IS STUCK IN
THE LAB OF HER CREATOR, THE EVIL SCIENTIST. TO ESCAPE, SHE CONCOCTS
A SLEEP-INDUCING SOUP, BUT HE SUSPECTS AND MAKES HER TASTE IT FIRST.
SALLY DOESN'T GET TO SEE JACK'S TRIUMPHANT RETURN, DRIVING A SNOW-
MOBILE PACKED WITH CHRISTMAS SOUVENIRS. VERY EXCITED, JACK CALLS
FOR A TOWN MEETING TO TELL EVERYONE WHAT HE FOUND.

THE TOWN MEETING SONG

JACK

*There were objects so peculiar
They were not to be believed
All around things to tantalize my brain.
It's a world unlike anything I've ever seen
And as hard as I try . . .
I can't seem to describe
Like a most improbable dream . . .*

*But you must believe when I tell you this
It's as real as my skull, and it does exist.*
                    Here . . . Let me show you.

*This is a thing called a present.
The whole thing starts with a box . . .*

DEVIL, WEREWOLF, HARLEQUIN DEMON
   —A box?
            Is it steel?
—   Are there locks?
   —Is it filled with a pox?
—
   —How delightful, a pox!   A pox!

JACK
   If you please!!!

   Just a box with bright colored paper
   And the whole thing's topped with a bow.

Among the crowd at the town meeting (below) are the arrow-faced Devil (left), as well as the withered Winged Demon, Three Mr. Hydes popping out of each other's hats, and Harlequin Demon, with his head bobbling on top of his mouth (all opposite).

WITCHES 1 AND 2
—A bow?
    But why?
—   How ugly!
—What's in it?
—   What's in it?

JACK
That's the point of the thing, not to know!

CLOWN, CREATURE UNDER THE STAIRS, UNDERSEA GAL
—It's a bat.
    Will it bend?
—It's a rat.
    Will it break?
—Perhaps it's the head that I found in the lake.

The Mayor shows his optimistic side.

The Mayor of Halloweenland is a large, frantic character with a tendency toward verbosity and an indecisive manner. "Jack! Please!" the Mayor cries at one point. "I'm only an elected official here! I can't make decisions by myself!"

The Mayor is—literally—two-faced. When he's confident, his face beams with a self-satisfied smile. When in doubt, his head whirls around to reveal a mask of dismay.

Verbose? Indecisive? Two-faced? A character like the Mayor could only exist in a fantasy world like Halloweenland. You'd never find a politician like that in real life.

The Cyclops is truly an alien creature (in a preliminary color design, opposite). Here Jack shows the Halloween citizens a present and is immediately buzzed with questions by the Witches. Below, as the storyboard tells it, he enthusiastically displays a stocking— to be met with a similar response.

JACK

> *Listen now, you don't understand.*
> *That's not the point of Christmasland.*
> *Now, pay attention . . .*
>
> *Now we pick up an oversized sock . . .*
> *And hang it like this on the wall.*

THREE MR. HYDES

> *—Oh yes! Does it still have a foot?*
> *—Let me see . . .*
>   *Let me look . . .*
> *—Is it rotted and covered with gook?*

JACK

> Let me explain.
>
> *There's no foot inside, but there's candy,*
> *And sometimes it's filled with small toys.*

The Corpse Dad (shown in a preliminary color study below) and the other characters shudder with delight as Jack tells them about the horrors of Sandy Claws (in the storyboard on bottom).

MUMMY, WINGED DEMON, CORPSE KID
   —Small toys!
   —   Do they bite?
   —   Do they snap?
   —Or explode in a fright?
   —Or perhaps they just spring out and
     Scare girls and boys.

MAYOR
   What a splendid idea—
   This Christmas sounds fun.
   Why I fully endorse it!
   Let's try it at once!

JACK
   Everyone, please, now not so fast.
   There's something here that you don't quite grasp.
    [speaks to himself as crowd grumbles]
   Well, I may as well give them
   what they want.

   And the best, I must confess,
     I have saved for the last
   For the ruler of this Christmasland . . .
     Is a fearsome king with a deep mighty voice
   Least, that is what I've come to understand.

   And I've also heard it told
   That he's something to behold
   Like a lobster, huge and red . . .
   And sets out to slay with his raingear on,
   Carting bulging sacks with his big great arms . . .
   That is, so I've heard it said.

   And on a dark, cold night
     Under full moonlight
   He flies off into a fog
     Like a vulture in the sky . . .
   And they call him—Sandy Claws.

CROWD
OOOOH . . . .

JACK (to himself)
Well, at least they're excited,
But they don't understand
That special kind of feeling
. . . In Christmasland.

Evil Scientist

Dr. Finklestein is the Evil Scientist of Halloweenland. His face resembles that of some kind of mutant duck, and the top of his head is a metal plate, which he throws back at will to absentmindedly scratch his brain. This mad genius scurries about in a motorized wheelchair.

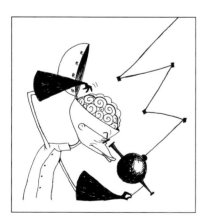

The creator of Sally, Dr. Finklestein is also her jailer. But despite his determination to hold her prisoner, he seems unable to stop her frequent escapes. She repeatedly slips deadly nightshade into his food, putting him into a deep sleep.

"Early on, I saw a drawing that someone had done," says Caroline Thompson. "It was of a scientist in a wheelchair with his head off, scrambling his own brains. I thought it was charming. And I wanted Sally to have an obstacle between her and Jack that was visible as opposed to emotional. So I folded the Evil Scientist into the subplot."

The Evil Scientist's lab suggests futuristic explorations and medieval mysteries, both outside (top) and inside (above).

UP IN HIS TOWER JACK STUDIES BOOK AFTER BOOK ABOUT CHRISTMAS, TRYING TO LEARN ITS SECRETS. HE BORROWS EQUIPMENT FROM THE EVIL SCIENTIST AND EXPERIMENTS, MAKING NOTES AND SCRIBBLING EQUATIONS ON A BLACKBOARD. ACROSS TOWN SALLY, LOCKED IN HER ROOM, WATCHES JACK'S LIGHT BURNING. DETERMINED TO BE FREE, SHE JUMPS OUT THE WINDOW. SHE THEN PICKS UP THE PIECES, SEWS HERSELF TOGETHER, AND MOVES CLOSER TO JACK. SOON A CROWD BEGINS TO GATHER, SINGING: "SOMETHING'S UP WITH JACK."

JACK'S OBSESSION

JACK

Christmastime is buzzing in my skull.
Will it let me be? I cannot tell.
There're so many things I cannot grasp . . .
When I think I've got it, then at last
Through my bony fingers it does slip
Like a snowflake in a fiery grip.

Something's here I'm not quite getting
Though I try, I keep forgetting
Like a memory long since past
Here in an instant, gone in a flash . . .
What does it mean? What does it mean?

In these little bric-a-brac,
A secret waiting to be cracked.
These dolls and toys confuse me so . . .
Confound it all—I love it, though!

Simple objects nothing more
But something's hidden through the door.
Though I do not have the key,
Something's there I cannot see.
What does it mean? What does it mean?

Jack examines specimens of Christmas toys, trying to discover their secrets, and struggles with a formula to bring it all together (shown here in preliminary concept sketches).

Sandy Claws = Christmas

replace
stockings stuffers

I've read these Christmas books so many times
I know the stories and I know the rhymes
I know the Christmas carols all by heart . . .
My skull's so full, it's tearing me apart.
As often as I read them, something's wrong . . .
So hard to put my bony finger on . . .

Or perhaps it's really not as
Deep as I've been led to think.
Am I trying much too hard . . . ?
Of course! I've been too close to see!
The answer's right in front of me!

It's simple really, very clear,
Like music drifting in the air
Invisible but everywhere.
Just because I cannot see it
Doesn't mean I can't believe it.

You know I think this Christmas thing—
It's not as tricky as it seems.
And why should they have all the fun?
It should belong to anyone . . .
Not anyone, in fact, but me!
Why, I could make a Christmas tree.
And there's no reason I can find
That I couldn't handle Christmastime.

I bet I could improve it too!
And that's exactly what I'll do!

EUREKA!

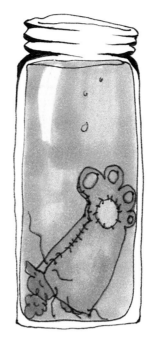

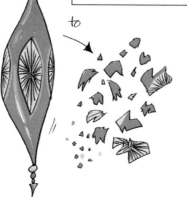

High up in his tower, Jack spends the night studying his Christmas artifacts under the light of the moon and gargoyle fixtures (in preliminary sketches, opposite). When he snips out a snowflake, he gets a spider. Using equipment borrowed from the Evil Scientist, he tests the composition of ornaments and toys (shown in the storyboard and early prop concepts above).

JACK QUICKLY ENLISTS THE AID OF EVERYONE IN HALLOWEENLAND TO HELP MAKE CHRISTMAS. CALLING DR. FINKLESTEIN TO THE FRONT OF THE LINE, JACK GIVES HIM THE TASK OF CONSTRUCTING REINDEER AND A FLYING SLEIGH. THEN HE TURNS TO LOCK, SHOCK, AND BARREL, THREE IMPISH CREATURES KNOWN AS "OOGIE BOOGIE'S BOYS." THEY GATHER IN A HUDDLE AND JACK WHISPERS WHAT HE HAS IN MIND.

Lock, Shock, and Barrel sport their characteristic grins in the final color design below. Their playthings (shown in preliminary sketches here) are just the opposite of Christmas toys.

THE SCHEMING SONG

LOCK, SHOCK, AND BARREL
   Kidnap Mr. Sandy Claws . . . ?

LOCK
   I wanna do it . . .

BARREL
      . . . Let's draw straws.

SHOCK
   Jack said we should work together.
   Three of a kind . . .

                  LOCK, SHOCK, AND BARREL
                        . . . Birds of a feather.
                  Now and forever . . .
                              . . . Weeee!
                  (La, la, la, la, etc.)

      Kidnap the Sandy Claws, lock him up real tight
      Throw away the key and then
      Turn off all the lights.

LOCK

First we're going to set some bait
Inside a nasty trap and wait.

SHOCK

When he comes a-sniffing we will
Snap the trap and close the gate.

LOCK

Wait! I've got a better plan
To catch this big red lobster man.
Let's pop him in a boiling pot
And when he's done we'll butter him up!

Lock, Shock, and Barrel are a tiny trio of mischievous trick-or-treaters who travel around in a walking bathtub. Lock wears a devil mask, Shock sports a witch mask, and Barrel has a ghoul mask. But when they take their masks off, they look exactly the same as before.

Usually, the scheming trio works for the villainous Oogie Boogie, but they undertake a delicate mission for Jack Skellington—to kidnap Santa Claus. The three little demons are beside themselves with glee. Together, they fiendishly think up all the horrible ways they can trap "the big red lobster man." They are going to have lots of fun.

LOCK, SHOCK, AND BARREL
Kidnap the Sandy Claws
Throw him in a box
Bury him for ninety years
And then see if he talks.

SHOCK
Then Mr. Oogie Boogie Man
Can take the whole thing over then.
He'll be so pleased I do declare
That he will cook him rare . . .

LOCK, SHOCK, AND BARREL
Weeee!

Lock, Shock, and Barrel live in a treehouse (below right). That's where they merrily plot just how to kidnap Sandy Claws (below).

Lock

> *I say that we take a cannon*
> *Aim it at his door and then*
> *Knock three times and when he answers*
> *Sandy Claws will be no more.*

Shock

> *You're so stupid, think now—*
> *If we blow him up to smithereens,*
> *We may lose some pieces and then*
>   *Jack will beat us black and green.*

Lock, Shock, and Barrel

> *Kidnap the Sandy Claws*
> *Tie him in a bag*
> *Throw him in the ocean*
> *And then see if he is sad.*

Lock and Shock

> *Because Mr. Oogie Boogie is the meanest guy around,*
> *If I were on his Boogie list, I'd get out of town.*

Barrel

> *He'll be so pleased by our success*
> *That he'll reward us too I bet.*
> *Perhaps he'll make his special brew*
> *Of snake and spider stew . . .*

Lock, Shock, and Barrel

> *. . . MMMMMMM . . . !*

Lock

> *We're his little henchmen and*

Barrel

>   *we take our job with pride.*
> *We do our best to please him, and stay on his good side.*

Shock

> *I wish my cohorts weren't so dumb . . .*

Lock (the puppet on top) has a devilish look, with or without his mask. The trick-or-treaters' cupboard (in a preliminary color study above) is full of deadly delights.

BARREL
I'm not the dumb one . . .

LOCK
. . . You're no fun.

SHOCK
Shut up.

Their scheme worked out, Lock, Shock, and Barrel pile into their walking bathtub, ready to take off on their mission.

LOCK
Make Me!

SHOCK
I've got something, listen now,
This one is real good, you'll see.
We'll send a present to his door
Upon there'll be a note to read.

Now in the box, we'll wait and hide
Until his curiosity
Entices him to look inside . . .

BARREL
And then we'll have him, one, two, three!

LOCK, SHOCK, AND BARREL
Kidnap the Sandy Claws, beat him with a stick . . .
Lock him up for ninety years and see what makes
him tick.

Kidnap the Sandy Claws, tie him in a knot
Put him in a coffin, how we'd like to see him rot.

Kidnap the Sandy Claws . . . Chop him into bits
Mr. Oogie Boogie is sure to get his kicks.

Kidnap the Sandy Claws . . . See what we will see,
Lock him in a cage and then throw away the key.

WAITING IN LINE FOR HER ASSIGNMENT, SALLY LOOKS WORRIED. WHEN JACK ASKS HER TO MAKE A SANTA OUTFIT, SHE TRIES TO VOICE HER DOUBTS ABOUT THE WHOLE VENTURE. BUT JACK IS FAR TOO EXCITED TO LISTEN. JUST THEN LOCK, SHOCK, AND BARREL SCURRY IN, SHOUTING, "WE'VE GOT HIM!" THEY OPEN UP THEIR SACK—AND OUT HOPS THE EASTER BUNNY. JACK ANGRILY SENDS THEM OFF AGAIN TO GET IT RIGHT, WHILE EVERYONE ELSE WORKS BUSILY AT THE HALLOWEEN FACTORY . . .

When Halloween makes Christmas, it has its own special look (as seen in the still above left and the prop designs here).

MAKING CHRISTMAS

MAYOR (optimist)
Making Christmas, making Christmas is so fine

CLOWN WITH TEARAWAY FACE
It's ours this time

MAYOR (optimist)
and won't the children be surprised

GROUP
It's ours this time

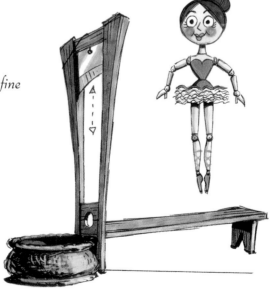

CORPSE CHILD
Making Christmas

MUMMY
Making Christmas

MUMMY AND CORPSE CHILD
Making Christmas

WITCHES
Time to give them something fun

WITCHES AND CREATURE LADY
They'll talk about for years to come.

MAYOR (optimist)
Let's have a cheer from every<u>one</u>

GROUP
It's time to party

DUCK TOY
Making Christmas, making Christmas.

Dying wreaths and strings of skulls are Halloweenland's idea of yuletide decor. The Witches load up their broomsticks with baskets of Christmas "treats" (shown in the prop designs below).

The Clown with the Tearaway Face merrily stuffs cat-o'-lanterns in boxes (on the set at left and in the storyboard below). Sally stitches Jack's Santa outfit in her sewing tent (in a preliminary concept drawing below).

VAMPIRES
>*Snakes and mice . . . get wrapped up so nice*
>*With spider legs . . . and pretty bows.*

VAMPIRES AND WINGED DEMON
>*It's ours this time.*

CORPSE FATHER
>*All together, that and this . . .*

CORPSE FATHER AND WEREWOLF
>*With all our tricks we're . . .*

CORPSE FATHER, WEREWOLF, AND DEVIL
>*. . . making Christmastime.*

WEREWOLF
>*Here comes Jack.*

JACK

I don't believe what's happening to me—
My hopes, my dreams . . . my fantasies.

HARLEQUIN DEMON

Won't they be impressed, I am a genius
See how I transformed this old rat
Into a most delightful hat.

JACK

My compliments from me to you
On this your most intriguing hat
Consider, though, this substitute . . .
A bat in place of this old rat.

NO, NO, NO, now that's all wrong.
This thing will never make a present.
It's been dead now for much too long
Try something fresher, something pleasant!
Try again. Don't give up!

THREE MR. HYDES

All together, that and this
With all our tricks we're making
Christmastime.

Sally is the only one with doubts. Although she follows Jack's wishes in creating a Santa outfit, she's really not at all sure about this whole Christmas venture.

60

*T*he Behemoth (above left) sings of his delight in Christmas in a storyboard drawing (which was later cut from the film), while the Corpse Dad (above) almost gets devoured by his toy. Igor (left, in a preliminary color study) helps the Evil Scientist with his tasks, receiving doggy treats as a reward.

MAN UNDER THE STAIRS

Christmas presents really are the biggest thrill
Inside each box a mystery
A million ways to fill this thing—
And then I think I've done the best

The Clown's cat-o'-lantern (below) and the Corpse Child's wrecked car (right) are real miniature objects in the movie, but they started out on the drawing board.

BEHEMOTH
    And each is prettier than the next.
    Making Christmas . . .

CREATURES AND BEHEMOTH (alternating)
    Making Christmas
    Making Christmas
    Making Christmas
    Making Christmas
    Making Christmas

SEVERED HEAD
    It's a real neat thing!

GROUP
    Making Christmas, making Christmas, la la la . . .
    It's almost here

GROUP AND WEREWOLF
    and we can't wait

GROUP AND HARLEQUIN DEMON
    So ring the bells and celebrate

GROUP
    'Cause when the full moon starts to climb
    We'll all sing out . . .

JACK
    It's—Christmastime!

SANTA IS GOING OVER HIS "NAUGHTY OR NICE" LIST WHEN THE DOOR-
BELL RINGS. THE MINUTE HE OPENS THE DOOR, THREE LITTLE DEMONS
SHOUT "TRICK OR TREAT!" AND STUFF HIM IN A SACK. THEY BRING SANTA
STRAIGHT TO JACK, WHO HAPPILY TELLS SANTA THAT HE WILL DELIVER ALL
THE PRESENTS THIS YEAR. AFTER JACK ADMONISHES LOCK, SHOCK, AND
BARREL TO TREAT SANTA WELL, THEY HURRY HIM OFF TO OOGIE BOOGIE'S
DARK LAIR.

TRYING TO STOP JACK'S ILL-CONCEIVED SCHEME, SALLY CREATES A
THICK FOG. ALL SEEMS LOST UNTIL ZERO'S SHINING PUMPKIN NOSE APPEARS
IN THE MIST AND HE TAKES THE LEAD, GUIDING JACK'S SLEIGH. DEJECTED,
SALLY WALKS AWAY FROM THE CHEERING THRONG.

Jack is delighted with his Santa attire, but Sally is convinced it's all wrong. Although Jack agrees something is missing (Santa's cap, as he later discovers), he's too excited to really hear what Sally has to say.

SALLY'S SONG

SALLY

*I sense there's something in the wind
That feels like tragedy's at hand,
And though I'd like to stand by him,
Can't shake this feeling that I have
The worst is just around the bend.*

*And does he notice my feelings for him?
And will he see how much he means to me?
I think it's not to be.*

*What will become of my dear friend?
Where will his actions lead us then?
Although I'd like to join the crowd
In their enthusiastic cloud,
Try as I may, it doesn't last.*

*And will we ever end up together?
No, I think not. It's never to become . . .
. . . For I am not the one . . .*

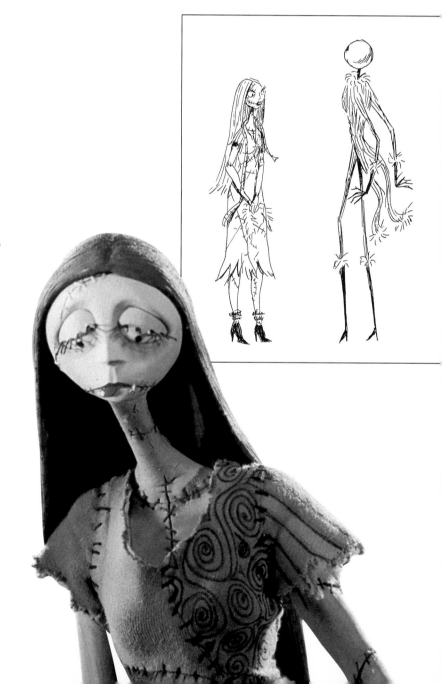

Jack is in seventh heaven, delivering presents to children in house after house. He doesn't realize that his presents are so ghastly that they terrify everyone. Panic spreads as one child receives a shrunken head and another watches a monster toy devour a Christmas tree. Jack, flying high above, is delighted. Meanwhile in a creepy dungeon, Santa is brought face to face with that gigantic walking bag of nasty stuff, Oogie Boogie.

Jack's coffin sleigh (in the design above) is filled with gifts, but when he cheerfully presents one to Timmy (right), it's a bit more of a surprise than the child expects (see storyboard, above right).

Howie runs away from his grinning Jack-in-the-box (below), while the Infant (bottom) stares in horror as his toy stuffs itself.

Tim Burton's sketch of Oogie was used for a color study (below). One-armed bandits (bottom) were designed for Oogie's lair.

OOGIE BOOGIE'S SONG (YOU'RE JOKING)

OOGIE BOOGIE
Well, well, well, what have we here?
Sandy Claws, huh? Ohhhh, I'm really scared.
So you're the one everybody's talkin' about. Ha, ha . . .

You're jokin', you're jokin'
I can't believe my eyes
You're jokin' me, you gotta be
This can't be the right guy—
He's ancient, he's ugly
I don't know which is worse . . .
I might just split a seam now if I don't die laughing first.

Even in Halloweenland, where the dreadful is commonplace, Oogie Boogie is particularly ghastly. He is a huge burlap sack bulging with spiders and snakes and creepy-crawlies. He has a sinister, gravelly voice, a voracious appetite, an appreciation for a pretty leg (even an unattached one), and a fondness for doing his slinky,

Cab Calloway–like dance.

Oogie Boogie did not appear in Tim Burton's original poem, but Burton later sketched a portrait of a weird potato-sack guy with horrible things inside. Yet Oogie remained a villain without a cause. Finding the right personality for him was hard, recalls Thompson. "We really counted on Danny's song to define Oogie's character."

Filled with bugs, Oogie Boogie represents the ultimate Halloween nightmare. And he was monstrous to the animators, too. The Oogie puppet is two feet high—gigantic for a stop-motion character.

Most of the other

puppets are only about half Oogie's height.

Animator Mike Belzer says, "I had to dig in with my feet and physically push the Oogie Boogie puppet. He's so huge and there's so much foam, therefore the armature needs to be very tight; it's literally wrestling with the puppet."

A scary guy has to live in a scary place, and Oogie's lair is a creepy gambling den, lit with eerie ultraviolet hues. Scattered about are gleaming torture devices, including an Iron Maiden that, true to the gambling theme, looks like the deadliest Queen of Spades on record. Artist Kelly Asbury indicates that while the rest of Halloweenland is "sort of fun scary," Oogie's lair is meant to have "a really threatening, sinister quality."

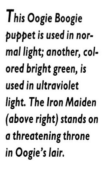

This Oogie Boogie puppet is used in normal light; another, colored bright green, is used in ultraviolet light. The Iron Maiden (above right) stands on a threatening throne in Oogie's lair.

When Mr. Oogie Boogie says there's trouble close at hand
You'd better pay attention now 'cause I'm the Boogie man!
And if you aren't shakin' then there's something very wrong
'Cause this may be the last time that you hear the Boogie Song.

OOGIE BOOGIE, THREE BATS, AND SEVEN LIZARDS (alternating)
Ohhhhh . . . . / Ohhhhh . . . . / Ohhhhh . . . .
Ohhhhh . . . . / Ohhhhh . . . . / Ohhhhh . . . .

OOGIE BOOGIE
I'm the Oogie Boogie Man.

Well if I'm feelin' antsy and I've nothin' much to do
I might just cook a special batch of snake and spider stew.
And don't ya know the one thing that would make it work so nice?
A roly-poly Sandy Claws to add a little spice.

Ohhhhh . . . . Whoa Ya . . . Whoa

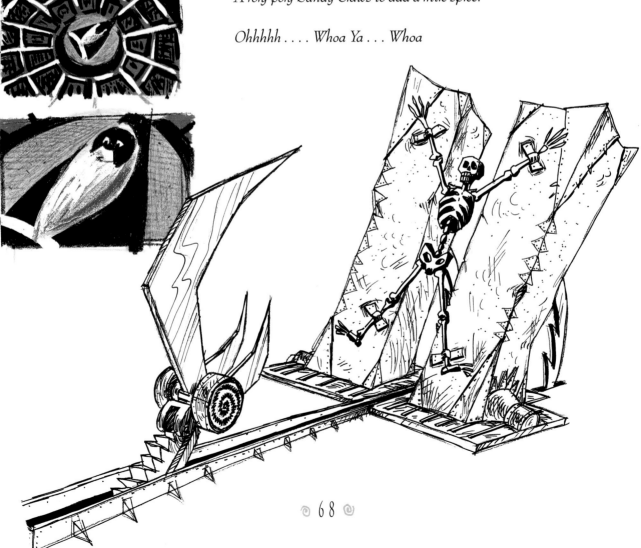

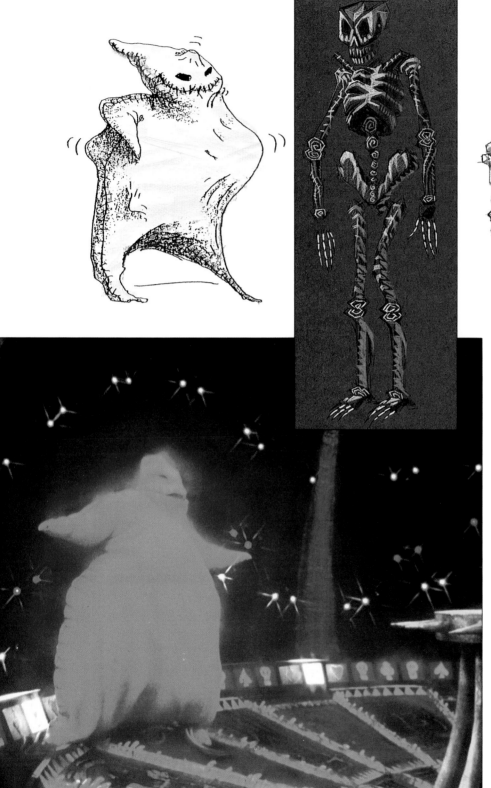

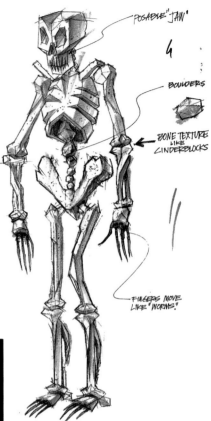

POSABLE "JAW"

BOULDERS

BONE TEXTURE
LIKE
CINDERBLOCKS

FINGERS MOVE
LIKE "WORMS."

Oogie ties Santa to his roulette wheel (in the storyboard color key, opposite left) and starts rolling dice. Santa can only stare in horror at the skeletons and torture devices that decorate Oogie's lair (shown in design sketches here). On the set (left) Oogie sings his song under ultraviolet light. He's similar but different from the colored-in version of Tim Burton's sketch (above left).

THREE SKELETONS, OOGIE BOOGIE, AND THREE BATS (alternating)
Ohhhhh . . . / Oh Yeah . . . / Ohhhhh . . .
He's the Oogie Boogie Man.

SANTA
Release me now or you must face the dire consequences
The children are expecting me so please come to your
senses.

OOGIE BOOGIE
You're jokin', you're jokin'
I can't believe my ears.
Would someone shut this fella up
I'm drownin' in my tears.
It's funny, I'm laughing . . .
You really are too much—
And now, with your permission,
I'm going to do my stuff.

SANTA
What are you going to do?

OOGIE BOOGIE
I'm gonna do the best I can . . . [dances]

The sound of rollin' dice to me is music in the air
'Cause I'm a gamblin' Boogie Man, although I don't play fair
It's much more fun, I must confess, when lives are on the line.
Not mine, of course, but yours, old boy, now that'd be just fine.

After asking Santa's "permission," Oogie really takes off and does his stuff (in story-board color keys at top). Finding the right look for Oogie was difficult. One concept (above) shows Oogie in stained, mildewy fabric. In Oogie's lair the Iron Maiden has an icy look in real light (in the color study, opposite center). Oogie appears threatening no matter what light he's in—especially if he's angry, as he is after discovering Sally's ruse to help Santa (opposite).

SANTA
Release me fast or you will have to answer for this heinous act.

OOGIE BOOGIE
Oh brother, you're something
You put me in a spin . . .
You aren't comprehending
The position that you're in.
It's hopeless, you're finished
You haven't got a prayer . . .
'Cause I'm Mr. Oogie Boogie
And you ain't going nowhere . . .

Ha Ha Ha Ha Ha!

SALLY SNEAKS IN TO RESCUE SANTA. LEAVING ONE LEG BY THE DOOR TO DISTRACT OOGIE, SHE TRIES TO UNTIE SANTA'S BONDS. BUT OOGIE CATCHES THEM BEFORE THEY ESCAPE. HE OPENS HIS MOUTH AND, LIKE A MONSTER VACUUM CLEANER, SUCKS THEM IN. UP IN THE SKY, JACK THINKS THAT PEOPLE ARE SETTING OFF FIREWORKS TO CELEBRATE HIS REMARKABLE CHRISTMAS. SUDDENLY, HE REALIZES THAT THE ROCKETS ARE AIMED AT HIM. HIS SLEIGH IS HIT, AND SHOUTING, "MERRY CHRISTMAS TO ALL AND TO ALL A GOOD NIGHT!," JACK PLUNGES TO THE GROUND.

POOR JACK

JACK

> *What have I done? What have I done?*
> *How could I . . . be so blind?*
> *All is lost . . . where was I?*
>
> *Spoiled all . . . spoiled all . . .*
> *Everything's . . . gone all wrong.*
>
> *What have I done? What have I done?*
> *Find a deep cave to hide in.*
> *In a million years they'll find me*
> *Only dust . . . and a plaque*
> *That reads here lies <u>Poor Old Jack!</u>*

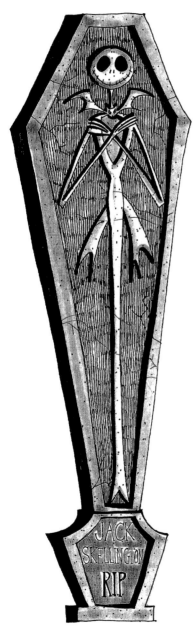

But I never intended all this madness . . . never
And nobody really understood . . . how could they?
That all I ever wanted was to bring 'em something great!
Why does nothing ever turn out like it should?

WELL . . . what the heck, I went and did my best
And, by God, I really tasted something swell.
For a moment, why, I even touched the sky
And at least I left some stories they can tell . . . I did.

And for the first time since I don't remember when
I felt just like my old bony self again.

And I, Jack . . . the Pumpkin King . . .
<u>That's right! I AM the Pumpkin King! . . . HA!</u>

And I just can't wait until next Halloween
'Cause I've got some new ideas that will make them scream
And, by God, I'm gonna give it all my might!
I hope there's time to set things right!

Jack tries to fly higher and higher in the sky to avoid the blasts (shown in the color key for the shot, above). But he can't escape, falling down, in tatters, into the arms of an angel on the ground (opposite bottom). In Halloweenland everyone mourns the passing of Jack, evidenced by a new tombstone (in drawing opposite).

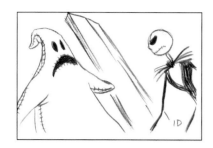

JACK ARRIVES IN OOGIE'S LAIR JUST BEFORE A HUGE BLADE SLICES THROUGH SALLY AND SANTA. A HAIR-RAISING BATTLE ENSUES. BUT OOGIE IS NO MATCH FOR JACK AND ENDS UP LITERALLY COMING UNRAVELED.

SANTA HURRIES OFF TO FIX CHRISTMAS, AND JACK—HOPING IT'S NOT TOO LATE—DEJECTEDLY WALKS HOME. THEN SNOW BEGINS TO FALL, BRINGING A SMILE TO JACK'S FACE. ALL AROUND HALLOWEENLAND CREATURES WONDER, "WHAT'S THIS?" ONLY SALLY IS SAD. SHE SITS ALONE IN THE CEMETERY, SINGING HER SONG. BUT THEN A SECOND VOICE JOINS HERS. IT IS JACK, ASKING HER TO SIT WITH HIM AND GAZE AT THE SKY.

Although Oogie's surprised to see Jack (he thought Jack was dead), he laughingly sets off his chopping machines (in storyboard above). Jack, however, is enraged and leaps into the fray (in color keys at right).

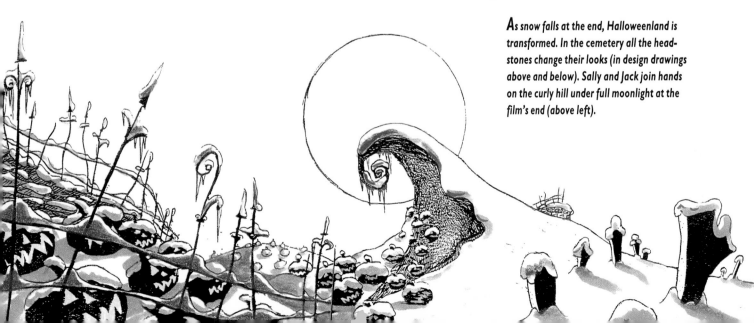

As snow falls at the end, Halloweenland is transformed. In the cemetery all the head-stones change their looks (in design drawings above and below). Sally and Jack join hands on the curly hill under full moonlight at the film's end (above left).

Tim Burton's Nightmare Before Christmas is, in the truest sense of the word, unique. Disney Chairman Jeffrey Katzenberg claims, "In the eight years I've been at the studio, the only other movie that really set out to do something unlike anything done before was *Who Framed Roger Rabbit?* I consider this to be a sister film."

The story of Jack Skellington's ill-conceived plan to take over Christmas delights people of every age. The weird and colorful supporting characters—Sally, Oogie Boogie, Lock, Shock, Barrel, and the others—inspire screams of laughter, and sometimes just screams. But *Nightmare Before Christmas* is a rarity in that the way it was produced is every bit as fascinating as the film itself. For audiences accustomed to animated films, *Nightmare Before Christmas* offers surprises in both style and technique. The characters are fanciful yet solid, three-dimensional beings. They move through a world that seems genuine, but could not exist in "real" life.

Although the completed film seems as effortless as a dream, it took years to reach the screen, requiring almost unimaginably detailed—sometimes tedious, sometimes impossible—creative effort. This is the story of how *Tim Burton's Nightmare Before Christmas* was made. It is told, to a great extent, in the words of the over 140 artists and technicians who brought the film to life.

The art of drawing is critical to Nightmare. *While jotting down his original poem, Tim Burton was already telling the story in his sketches (opposite). For the film, the art department's designs for props like Jack's bed (below) emphasized the graphic look Burton wanted. On screen, when Jack wanders through a forest (below right), the set has a three-dimensional presence and yet retains a drawn quality.*

ORIGINAL POEM

Tim Burton's original poem "The Nightmare Before Christmas," which was written more than a decade ago, is simplicity itself. It follows the adventures of Jack Skellington, who has grown very tired of scaring people and creating terror year after year for Halloween. When he discovers Christmas, he decides to become Santa Claus for one night—with disastrous results.

In its title, as well as many of its verses, Burton's poem loosely spoofs Clement Moore's classic that begins: "'Twas the night before Christmas." Overall, the poem's style suggests Dr. Seuss trapped in an Edgar Allan Poe epic. It is at once whimsical and dark, a tribute to the disturbed child within us all.

The poem begins:

It was late one fall in Halloween, the air had quite a chill,
And against the moon a skeleton sat alone upon the hill.
He was tall and thin with a bat bow tie,
Jack Skellington was his name.

Explaining how tired he is of the Halloween routine, Jack says:

"I'm bored with leering my horrible glances
And my feet hurt from doing skeleton dances."

As the poem continues, it is clear Jack is very unhappy.

Then out from a grave with a curl and a twist,
Whimpered and whined a spectral wist.
It was a little ghost dog, with a faint little bark,
With a jack-o'-lantern nose that glowed in the dark.

But even his dog Zero, the poem explains, cannot cheer up Jack, who walks sadly on and on through the dark forest for a night and a day. Then he discovers something that makes him stop—some unusual doors etched in the trees. With a bit of trepidation, he opens one door and immediately falls into Christmas Town. As Burton wrote:

Burton's quick sketches (below and opposite, center) clearly express the emotional content of the poem. Other drawings by Burton begin to detail the look of Jack and Christmas Town (opposite).

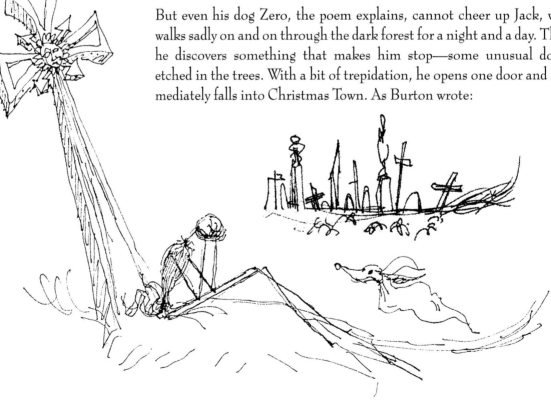

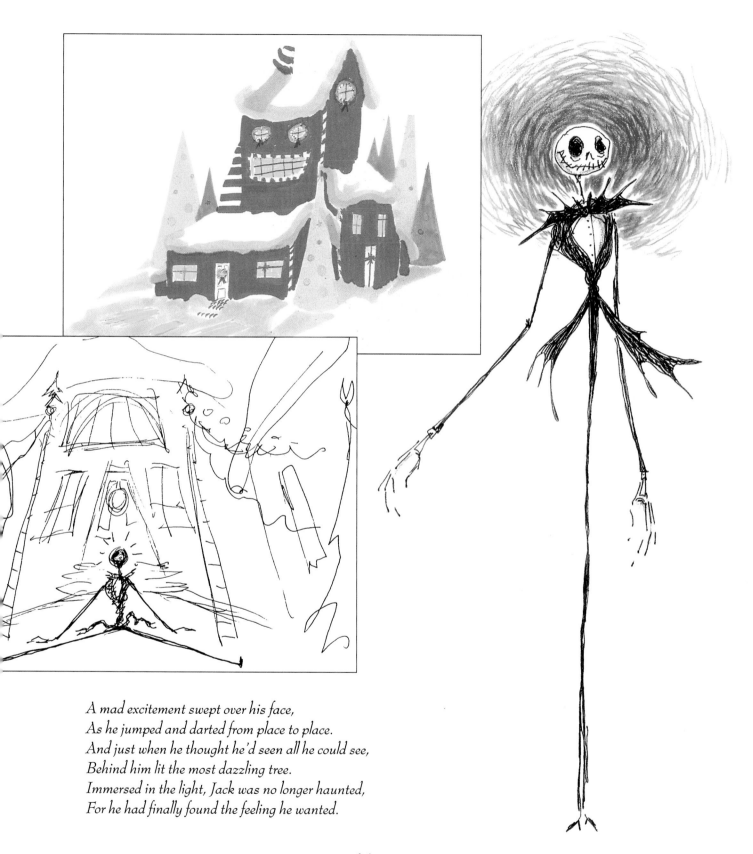

A mad excitement swept over his face,
As he jumped and darted from place to place.
And just when he thought he'd seen all he could see,
Behind him lit the most dazzling tree.
Immersed in the light, Jack was no longer haunted,
For he had finally found the feeling he wanted.

These and other drawings by Burton were the inspiration for set and character design in the film. Of course, no puppet could be as skinny as the drawing of Jack opposite, but when Jack appears as Santa on screen he creates a similar spidery impression.

Jack is determined to tell his Halloween friends about this wonderful place, so he gathers up a variety of souvenirs, including candy, toys, and even some snow. As the poem notes:

> Back in Halloween gathered a group of Jack's peers,
> And they stared in amazement at his Christmas souvenirs.
> For this wondrous vision none were prepared,
> Most were excited (though a few were quite scared).

Jack thinks and thinks about what he has seen. He feels it's unfair that Santa Claus gets to spread cheer, while all that he does is scare people and create fear. He believes it's time to set things right, so he takes action. The poem continues:

> In Christmas Town, Santa was working on toys,
> When at his workshop door, he heard a soft noise.
> He answered the door, and with startled surprise,
> He saw weird little creatures that were strangely disguised.

The tiny trick-or-treaters open up a huge sack, and before Santa knows what is happening to him, they shove him inside. Santa is brought to Halloween, where Jack explains that he is going to take over the role of Santa this year. By Christmas Eve Jack and his friends are ready with their version of Christmas, but a thick fog comes in and threatens to disrupt their plans. Then Jack notices Zero with his "nose so bright," and Zero takes the lead, guiding Jack's sleigh as it soars up into the sky. As the poem describes it:

> 'Twas the nightmare before Christmas and all through the house,
> Not a creature was peaceful, not even a mouse.
> The stockings all hung by the chimney with care,
> When opened that morning would cause quite a scare!
> The children who were nestled all snug in their beds,
> Would have nightmares of monsters and skeleton heads.

Instead of laughter, people hear groans. And Santa's bells sound like the rattle of bones. Even stranger is the sight of Jack, flying above in his "coffin sleigh," as:

> From house to house, with a true sense of joy,
> Jack happily issued each present and toy.

His presents are a bit macabre, including:

> A man-eating plant disguised as a wreath,
> And a vampire teddy bear with very sharp teeth.

When panic begins to take hold, Jack doesn't notice at first—he's "too much involved with his own Christmas spirit!" And even when he does notice, he thinks everyone is thanking him. But this is no celebration.

As the guns explode, Jack and Zero try to avoid them by flying higher in the sky:

> *And away they all flew like the storm of a thistle,*
> *Until they were hit by a well-guided missile.*

After Jack falls to the ground, he is grief-stricken, crying out:

> *"I thought I could be Santa, I had such belief."*

The poem ends, though, on a happier note. As Zero tries to turn himself into a handkerchief to dry Jack's tears, the two hear Santa's voice. Although Santa indicates that what Jack did was wrong, he realizes that Jack's intentions were good—and, "with a wink of his eye," he hurries off to deliver Christmas in the traditional way.

When Burton decided to take his poem and a handful of atmospheric drawings that he had made to accompany it and turn it all into a movie, he knew that the skeletal theme—like the hero Jack Skellington—needed a great deal of fleshing out. His original poem contained only three clear characters: Jack, his ghost dog Zero, and Santa Claus. While the spine of the story remained essentially the same, several important new characters were added for the film: Sally, who, like Jack, longs for a richer life; the horrible Oogie Boogie and his devilish little henchmen Lock, Shock, and Barrel; the two-faced Mayor of Halloween Town; and Dr. Finklestein, who created Sally—and wants to keep her prisoner.

By the time the film was completed, Burton's rhyming outline had become a funny and compelling mixture of love, horror, and redemption. Jack Skellington's search for identity contrasts with Sally's struggle to free herself from the Evil Scientist's clutches and to make Jack understand how good his life can be if he just accepts himself as he is.

Director Henry Selick says that even before the plot was developed and the theme expanded, *Nightmare Before Christmas* was fascinating. "Tim's basic story is elegant, simple, very strong," Selick notes. "Everyone wants to try on somebody else's shoes to try out another person's life for a change. *Nightmare* takes that idea to a fantastic level."

Screenwriter Caroline Thompson adds, "The film's sophistication is, ironically, in its simplicity. It is Jack's journey. He learns to recognize his own strengths. There's definitely a lesson to be learned. More or less, 'Be true to thyself.' That's where our joys are."

Burton's vision of Jack and Zero was clear from the start, although he did many drawings like the ones here to show their different moods. Santa gained a little weight from the initial sketch opposite to the one above, used for the film.

SONGS

In many musicals the songs are merely pleasant diversions, moments when the story pauses so that the stars can sing and dance for a while. Such moments can be magical. Or they can be intrusive and annoying. But the best, most durable musicals in the history of film and theater are those in which the songs are woven into the story and help to propel the plot with their lyrics, melodies, and mood.

The ten songs that Danny Elfman composed for *Nightmare Before Christmas* are of the latter variety. They are crucial to the film; the plot would make no sense without them. But Elfman's songs were important in another way: they actually helped the story—and then the script—take shape from the very beginning. Without Elfman's contribution, *Nightmare Before Christmas* would have been a vastly different film.

The process by which Elfman composed the songs for *Nightmare* is not the usual approach in modern Hollywood. "This is the way musicals were done in the thirties and forties," Elfman reflects. "Today you have a finished script and then think of ways to plug the songs in. But Tim and I started with a skeleton of a story—no pun intended—and developed a tone through the songs. It was a very organic way of developing a musical."

In the evolution of the story and songs of *Nightmare Before Christ-*

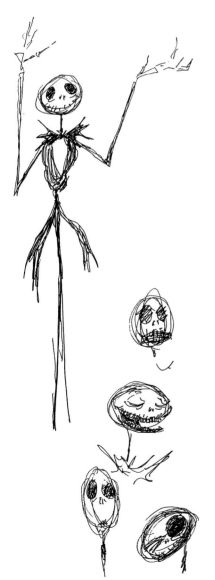

Tim Burton's sketches (below) helped give Danny Elfman a feeling for Jack's personality, which Elfman then brought out in composing the music and lyrics for songs like "What's This?" (below right).

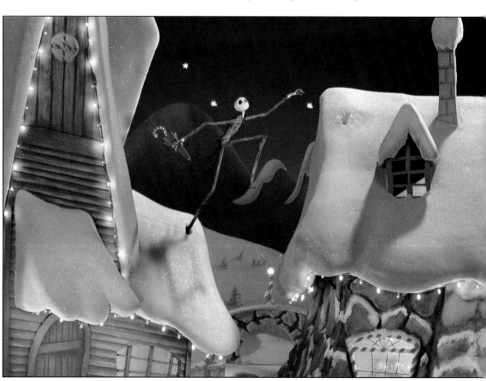

*U*sing Elfman's lyrics as their initial script, the storyboard artists gave the songs a visual form. In the excerpts from "The Town Meeting Song" at left, for example, their images show just how Jack excites the crowd with his tale of Christmas Town's "fearsome king." One eager listener is the Corpse Mom (shown in the final color design below).

mas, it is difficult to separate one from the other. They grew out of each other in a complex process of collaboration. Burton's story ideas triggered responses in Elfman, who then wrote the songs. The songs in turn suggested new story points to Caroline Thompson, whose revision of the script led Burton to alter and expand the original story.

"There was a period of time when we were all trying to figure out how to get started," says Elfman. "None of us had done a musical. Tim sent me a whole series of color drawings of Jack Skellington, the sleigh, and the reindeer. The drawings really got me going."

At this point there was no script; there wasn't even a completed story. Elfman and Burton began a series of meetings that Elfman feels, in retrospect, were an ideal way of working. Burton would visit Elfman, and they would discuss the story one scene at a time, talking about the tone and emotion. "As we were talking, I would begin to hear the music," Elfman recalls. "The instant Tim would leave I'd begin composing the song. Three days later, Tim would come over, I'd play him the song, and then we'd begin all over again on the next section."

At their meetings Elfman felt like a kid at story time, waiting to hear the next installment. When Burton described Jack's discovery of Christmas Town, Elfman went off to write "What's This?" (see pages 36–41)—underlining Jack's joy at finding "this wonderful new

A shot of Jack (right), Burton's drawing (below), a rendering of the Evil Scientist's lab (below right), a color key for Oogie's dance (bottom), and the Sally puppet (opposite) are just a few stages in making the film.

place." Then, at their next meeting, Elfman asked, "Now what happens?" Burton replied, "Well, Jack has to describe Christmas to Halloween Town." Then Elfman exclaimed, "Wait, I have a great idea for that!" And he hurried off to write "The Town Meeting Song" (pages 42–47).

"I wouldn't think past the next area of the story," Elfman recalls. "Sometimes I'd have to say to Tim, 'Please get out! I can hear the music and I have to get it down before I forget it.' What I'd get out of our conversations would carry right into the song. It was really fun. Before we knew it we had ten songs, and those ten songs told quite a bit of the story."

"Originally, Tim and Michael McDowell [the initial screenwriter] were going to write the lyrics and give Danny suggestions," says Caroline Thompson. She laughs. "By the third song he was so far ahead of them, they just said, 'Do it!'"

Elfman's songs helped some characters express themselves and established the personalities of others. While Burton created the character of Jack Skellington in his original poem, Elfman helped round out Jack's personality in songs like "Jack's Lament" (see pages 30–32).

Elfman took Burton's suggestion of the villainous Oogie Boogie and defined him through his song (performed by gravel-voiced Ken Page). Oogie Boogie's musical number (see pages 66–71) recalls the wonderful moments in Max and Dave Fleischer's Betty Boop cartoons of the thirties when Cab Calloway would wail a nasty blues tune like "Minnie the Moocher." Oogie even performs a slinky Callowayesque dance—not too easy when you're a huge burlap creature filled with crawling bugs.

The impish trick-or-treaters Lock, Shock, and Barrel also have their own song. So does Sally—although her song was written rather late in the composing process, after Caroline Thompson had been brought in to write the script. "Sally was a character that Danny took my lead on rather than the other way around," Thompson points out.

Not only do Elfman's songs help define the characters, but also no major plot point occurs without the accompaniment of music. In the strange lands of *Nightmare Before Christmas*, as in the sunnier Technicolor worlds of Hollywood's great musicals, the characters communicate to each other and to us through song.

SCRIPT

An initial, uncompleted version of the script for *Nightmare Before Christmas* was written by Michael McDowell, who had previously worked with Tim Burton on the ingenious, hilariously macabre *Beetlejuice* (1988). "The original draft had some good ideas," Selick says, "but it was not completely successful. We actually started the movie without a screenplay." Fortunately, Danny Elfman had already written the lyrics for the songs. As Selick explains, "The songs had a lot of storytelling within them so we tackled them first. We figured we could rework material later around the songs."

Caroline Thompson was brought in after storyboarding had begun. "When I came in," she says, "Danny Elfman's songs were about eighty percent written. My objective was to write a story to thread all these songs together. To fill out characters who weren't otherwise filled out."

"I never even saw the original script," she recalls. "They just gave me Danny's lyrics. I remember saying to Tim, 'Just let me take it away for a week and I'll see what I can bring back.' So I went up north for a

week, rented a house on the beach, wrote fifty pages, came back, and he was happy."

In addition to strengthening the storyline and fleshing out some of the characters, Thompson saw her first challenge as creating dialogue that would be true both to Burton's strange and wonderful drawings and to the Dr. Seussian tone of Elfman's lyrics. "I didn't want the dialogue to feel antithetical or goofy," Thompson says. "I wanted it to be in the spirit of the thing, so I tried to find some 'bent' rhymes."

As in most areas of this highly collaborative film, it is sometimes impossible to say who did what. Co-producer Kathleen Gavin says that the give-and-take of *Nightmare Before Christmas* demanded an involvement from Thompson that was more than that normally required from screenwriters. "Animation, perhaps more than live action, goes through an evolutionary process," explains Gavin. "There is a script, you start storyboarding, and you work out the action. Then you realize: 'Oh, that doesn't quite work,' so you go back and rewrite part of the script. In animation you have to have writers who are willing and interested in being part of the process, and fortunately for us, Caroline was. You really need the writer to be involved while you're boarding it because what you see on the screen is an amalgam of the work of the writer, storyboard artist, and director; it's very interactive."

"It required a lot of flexibility," Thompson agrees. "The script would go to the storyboard artists, and they would basically tear it apart. It no longer existed. It would become drawings with little subtitles and they would wing it. Then I would see the drawings and wing it back." Yet, even with all this back and forth, Thompson notes, "The basic structure of the script remained what I gave them after that initial week of work."

Throughout the entire production of *Nightmare Before Christmas*, the screenplay was a living, growing thing. "My relationship to it wasn't completely finished until all the dialogue had been recorded," Thompson comments. "I could never really sleep at night," she laughs. "I couldn't just say, 'Well, that one's done.' It was a very long process for everybody."

Although **Nightmare** has some spooky settings (suggested by the drawing of the graveyard below), it also has a lot of humor. Tim Burton's sketch of reindeer reading Edgar Allan Poe (above) hints at the combination of the playful and macabre evident in the shot of the earnest Behemoth pulling the Pumpkin King (opposite).

STORYBOARDS

The storyboard is absolutely crucial to the production of an animated film. It serves as the first visual version of the movie, telling the story blow by blow in a series of still pictures.

Usually, after the original story has been expanded into script form, a team of storyboard artists renders each scene in one or more sketches—sometimes highly detailed, sometimes merely symbolic. These drawings are pinned in sequence onto a series of large boards until the entire movie has been rendered in visual terms. For *Nightmare Before Christmas* about fifty boards, each containing some sixty-six drawings, were needed to tell the complete story.

On most animated films, the sequence from story to script to storyboard is relatively straightforward. But *Nightmare Before Christmas* rarely took the "normal" route. "We didn't have a full script when we started," says Joe Ranft, head of storyboarding, "so we started boarding the songs. Danny Elfman's songs are like miniature films in themselves. His song 'What's This?' was the first thing we boarded and the first thing that went into production."

When Caroline Thompson's first draft of the script arrived, Ranft, Mike Cachuela, Jorgen Klubien, and Bob Pauley boarded the entire film, beginning a series of exchanges that kept everything—script, storyboards, the film itself—in constant metamorphosis. "Caroline would

Production coordinator Jill Ruzicka and storyboard artist Mike Cachuela (above) discuss the storyboards for the sequence in which Jack delivers Christmas (shown close up, opposite). The first storyboard was done for the song "What's This?" (shown partially on the next two pages). Building on Burton's initial drawings and Elfman's lyrics, the storyboard artists contributed touches like Jack's bumping into a snowman and then popping inside him (not shown).

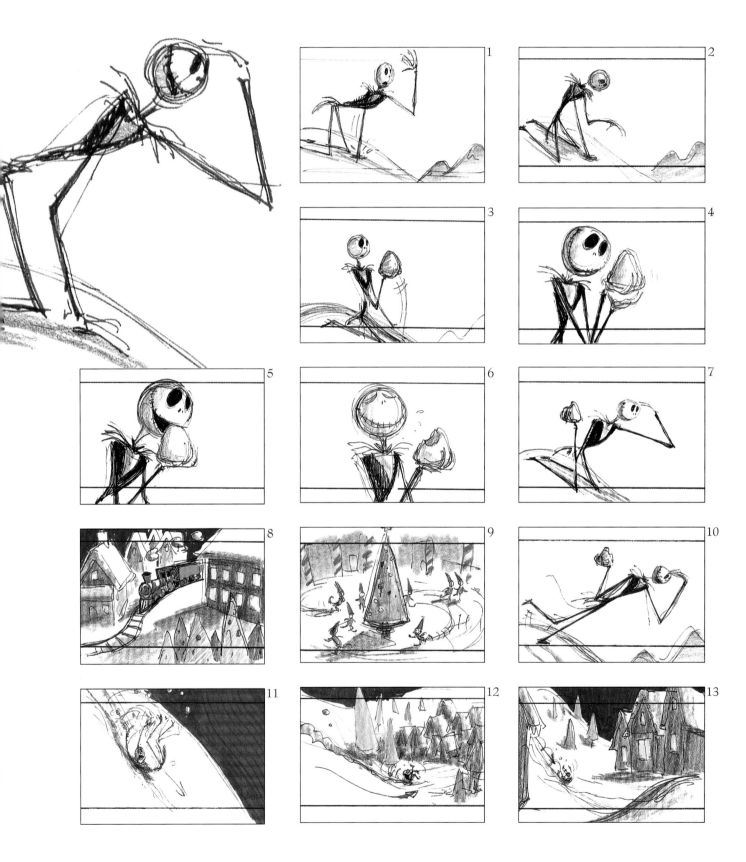

rewrite based on our drawings," indicates Ranft, "and we would re-board from her latest draft. Or we'd have an idea and do some drawings and fax them to her, and she'd write it into the script. It was a fun collaboration."

Cachuela remembers that the initial storyboard took between eight and twelve months to complete. "We would take Caroline Thompson's script," Cachuela explains, "and have a discussion with Henry Selick about how a scene should be approached. We'd do thumbnails—small sketches, rough sketches, enough to get the story across. We'd pin these up in rough order and Henry would come back and say, 'This is great' or 'This isn't what I wanted at all' or 'Just make a couple of changes here and there.'"

Although all animated films are worked out in storyboards, the demands of stop-motion require much more from the storyboarding department. "We rely heavily on our storyboards," emphasizes co-producer Kathleen Gavin, "for how many puppets we need, how many sets to

The basic storyboard for "Oogie Boogie's Song" was done in black and white (see page 176). But when it was decided to film this sequence in black, or ultraviolet, light—transforming Oogie's lair into a chamber of eerily glowing hues—the art department prepared the color key shown here to guide the painting and lighting of the sets.

Sandy Claws, huh? Ohhh, I'm really scared..."

OOGIE (O.S.): "So you're the one everybody's talkin' about... Ha, ha, ha, ha..."

OOGIE: "You're Jokin', You're Jokin', I can't believe my eyes. You're Jokin' me, you gotta be–This can't be the right guy. He's ancient, he's ugly, I don't Know which is worse..."

build, how many scenes take place in a certain area. Everything that happens subsequently is based completely on the storyboards."

Ranft agrees. For him, the purpose of the storyboard is to "convey an idea or an approach and hit the emotional core of it." He adds, "The animators then retranslate our drawings and, hopefully, make them better. It's like a relay race. We're the first baton and we try our best to get something up there that's entertaining and funny. But everyone else down the line takes it and improves on it."

The storyboard is where abstract ideas are first put into visual terms. It is also where experimentation takes place and mistakes can be made—inexpensively. "In live action they shoot coverage," says Ranft, "but in animation you don't have that luxury. In storyboarding you can at least try different versions of things."

Cachuela, however, stresses the need to be precise about details once the idea has taken shape. "Our animators don't have the luxury of just doing another drawing to correct a scene," he says. "If the angle isn't right, they may have to rebuild a whole set. It's cost prohibitive if you're not clear in the beginning."

Ranft interjects, "I didn't even know, at the beginning, what the problems were. Set guys would come up to me and say, '*See what your little drawings made us do?*' They might have had to build ten more feet on a set because of the angle I chose." In cel animation, Ranft clarifies, the artist simply paints a background. But in this kind of animation, the crew has to physically build the set under a tight deadline.

Overall, the storyboard artists have tremendous input into the way different sequences develop. But the director still has the final say. "It's his vision, incorporating our ideas," Cachuela notes. "We give him a variety of things to choose from, although every once in a while there's something that has to be really specific about character relationships or action in a scene. The storyboard department is basically Henry Selick's drawing hand."

Once the storyboard is complete, it is photographed by a movie camera, creating a "story reel." Each storyboard shot is edited to run the same length as the final shot in the film. The story reel is synched up to a temporary dialogue soundtrack and gradually transformed into a real movie. As each scene is animated, it is cut into the story reel in place of the sketches. Thus the filmmakers always have a reasonable facsimile of their movie—a kind of Frankenstein monster, part storyboard art, part completed animation. As Selick puts it, "You kind of make the film twice."

In preparing storyboards for scenes like the one below (where Jack discovers the holiday doors) or opposite (where Lock, Shock, and Barrel appear at Santa's door), the artists do much more than simply draw a picture. "We're really writing with our drawings," explains Jorgen Klubien. The panels not only tell the story, but give information about staging, props, and camera angles.

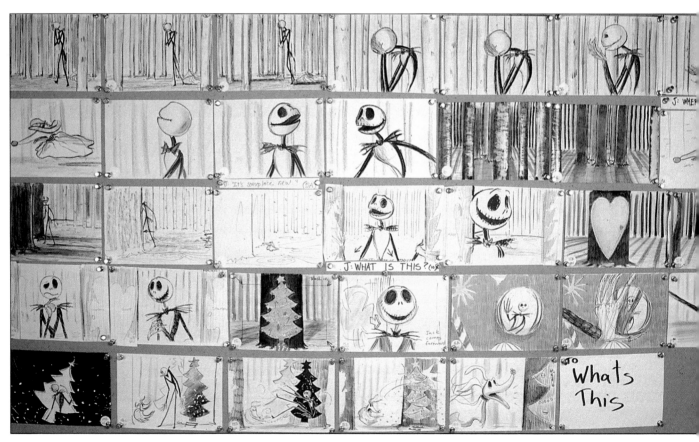

1

SANTA (O.S.)
Kathleen, Bobby, Susie ... Yes,

2

SFX paper ruffling

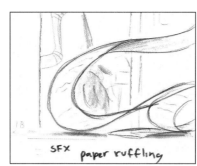

3

nice ... nice ... Naughty

4

nice...nice... There's Hardly
any naughty children This year

5

Ding! Dong!

SFX: Ding Dong!
SANTA: N....who could that be? (in)

6

SFX: Footsteps and Doorknob Turning.

7

LOCK, SHOCK & BARREL:
Trick or treat!

8

SANTA:
Huh?

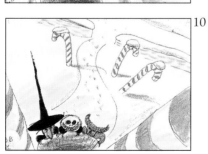

9

10

11

ART DIRECTION

If the storyboard department is where the film is first rendered in visual terms, the art department is where the initial sketches are turned into more fully realized concepts. The artists, headed by art director Deane Taylor, work from the storyboards and, perhaps more crucially in terms of style, from Tim Burton's drawings. "Tim's style is so distinct, so locked down and worked out," says Taylor. "We try not to lose any of that feeling, but instead try to work with it and enhance it."

Taylor and fellow artists Kelly Asbury, Kendal Cronkhite, and Bill Boes do everything necessary to imagine a three-dimensional world, making hundreds of two-dimensional sketches. They design sets and props, make color decisions, and work out design details. "We work on different conceptual ideas," explains Cronkhite. "Everything from what actual props and set pieces look like to color and lighting."

Once the concept is approved by Taylor and Selick, the artist does a complete illustration. This two-dimensional drawing is given to Boes or Gregg Olsson to be turned into a quarter-scale three-dimensional mockup. Eventually the drawings and mockups go to the model and set builders, who create full-size versions of the art department's designs.

While working on the three-dimensional mockups, Boes often gets new ideas. "Hey, what if we did this?" he may ask. There's a lively interchange among the artists. "We keep swapping ideas," Boes notes.

*T*im Burton's drawings of props like the tarantula chandelier in Jack's study (opposite, top left) or characters like the bass player (opposite, bottom right) are sometimes the direct source of inspiration for the art department's studies. Other designs (like the Halloween-style toy duck below) come out of storyboard concepts. Still other ideas develop on the drawing board, such as the early concept for a torture device in Oogie's lair that Deane Taylor is sketching at left.

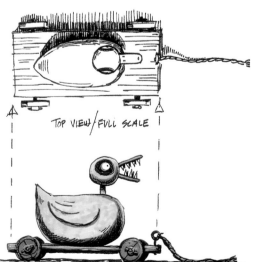

TOP VIEW / FULL SCALE

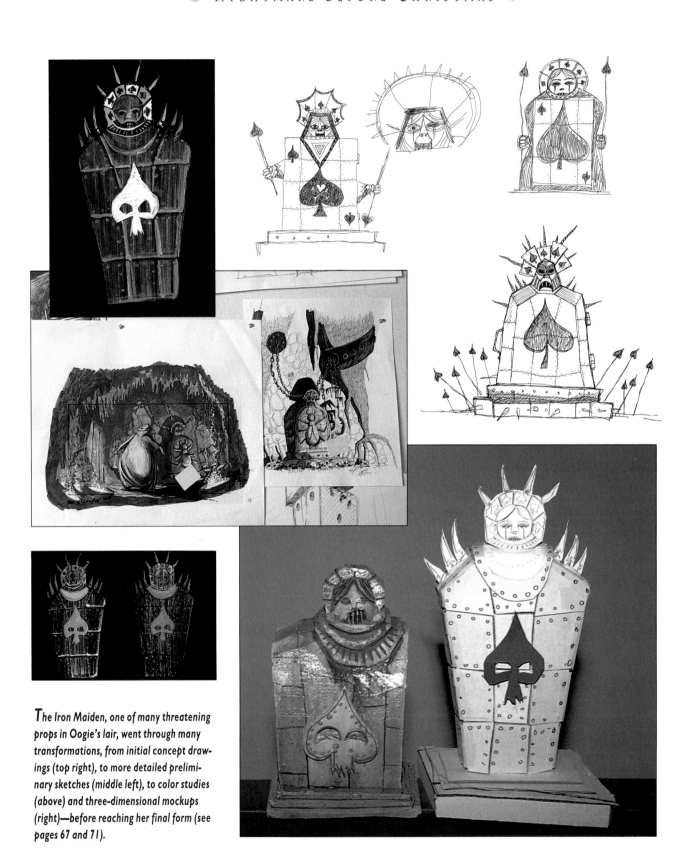

The Iron Maiden, one of many threatening props in Oogie's lair, went through many transformations, from initial concept drawings (top right), to more detailed preliminary sketches (middle left), to color studies (above) and three-dimensional mockups (right)—before reaching her final form (see pages 67 and 71).

Asbury points to a series of drawings on a wall depicting the terrifying Iron Maiden, a torture device in Oogie's gambling lair. He explains how the image of an Iron Maiden in the storyboard evolved into a large metal Queen of Spades reflecting "the gambling aspect of Oogie as well as his sinister, torturing side." According to Asbury, "The Iron Maiden started with drawings, then it went to Bill Boes, who built a cardboard mockup. Then Kendal Cronkhite elaborated on it again. All four of us in the art department had a hand in it at some point."

The interplay between two-dimensional and three-dimensional renderings of a concept is crucial, Taylor says, because the sets must do so much more than simply look good. "Technical considerations are major," Taylor stresses. "You have to think about getting the lights where you need them to be, about access for the animator. It's easy to draw a beautifully lit character, but if you can't get into the set to put the light there, you've lost your look."

The artist's job on any given set is not done until the scene has been shot and the set is no longer needed. Each artist checks as the set designers devise the blueprints and construct the piece in the shop. "If you see that some part of your drawing is not being translated correctly," Taylor says, "that's the time to jump in and change it, before it's cut out and nailed down."

After the set has been built, painted, and textured, the artist watches as it gets constructed on stage, doing the final tweaking: adjusting props, whatever. "You must make sure that it looks like your original drawing, based on Tim's style," insists Taylor.

Rick Heinrichs, the film's visual consultant, underlines the importance of its graphic look. He notes that even though the sets are three-dimensional, "they take advantage of very two-dimensional design elements."

The buildings, backgrounds, and trappings of *Nightmare*'s world show influences as diverse as Robert Wiene's *The Cabinet of Dr. Caligari* (1919) and ancient cave drawings. Creating this off-center environment led all the artists to, in Cronkhite's words, "push things as far as we could go."

"I had to design a treehouse at one point," says Asbury. "I would try to keep in mind the structure, but Henry Selick kept saying, 'It needs to look like it's about to fall off.' And I would just push it and push it until I thought, 'I don't know how they're going to build this.'" He laughs. "Well, it got built."

Lock, Shock, and Barrel's treehouse already looks precarious in the early concept drawing below, but it became even more rickety in later designs—presenting the set department with the challenge of building it.

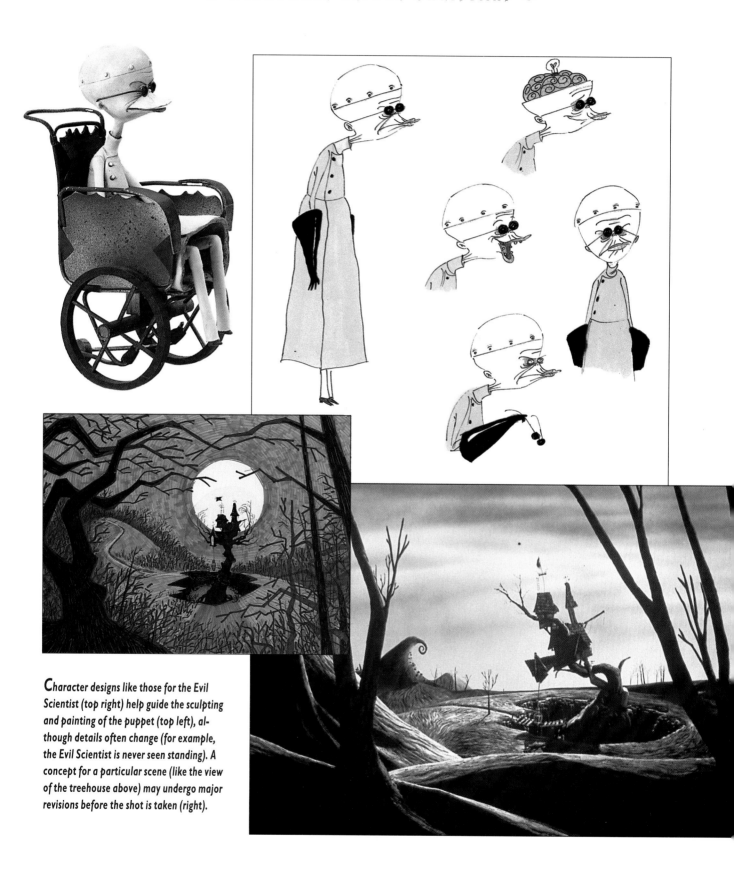

Character designs like those for the Evil Scientist (top right) help guide the sculpting and painting of the puppet (top left), although details often change (for example, the Evil Scientist is never seen standing). A concept for a particular scene (like the view of the treehouse above) may undergo major revisions before the shot is taken (right).

*T*he final rendering (left) of Lock, Shock, and Barrel's arrival at Santa's door adds detail to the storyboard (page 99), and it is followed for the setup of the shot (below left). The same is true of the illustration of Sally after she jumps out of her window (bottom), although the closeup (below) is at a different angle. In both drawings, the background is painted on paper as an empty set (without figures). The characters are placed on an acetate overlay and can be rearranged.

There are several drawings for every set in the film, from the Town Square during the post-Halloween celebration (right) to the Real World interiors on Christmas Eve (opposite). The artist usually draws the scene or a single prop (like the stocks below) in line first, using the medium-point felt-tip pen that Tim Burton favors. If the line drawing is approved by Henry Selick, it is photocopied, and the artist works with markers and colored pencils to try out different color possibilities.

To force himself into drawing things in surprising ways, Asbury, who is right-handed, started drawing with his left hand. "That's when I started getting it," he recalls. "It made everything just a little unsound."

"So we all started drawing with our left hands," Cronkhite interjects, laughing. "It worked completely. It was strange because it's more tentative and you do end up with things off-balance." Boes adds that he suspects "Tim Burton always draws with his opposite hand—and doesn't tell anybody!"

Although the art department devoted considerable attention to individual props such as the Iron Maiden, this was only a small part of their task. By far the most complex aspect of their job was the creation of the four distinct landscapes that make up *Nightmare*'s world.

"There's Christmas Town," says Cronkhite, "which is soft and sloppy. It's Dr. Seuss and bright colors, like candy. And then there's Halloweenland, which is German Expressionist, odd angles, on-edge, off-kilter."

Asbury adds that while Selick wanted Christmas Town to look soft and fluffy as if it were made of candy, "he wanted Halloweenland to be something that, if you ran your hand over it, it would cut you."

Cronkhite continues, "The Real World is a little bit Bauhaus, as well as 1950s to '60s, very rigid, designed isometrically." As Asbury puts it, "With its pastel primary colors, its rigidness and right angles, the Real World is almost weirder than Halloweenland."

The drawings above show three slightly different ideas for the street leading to the Evil Scientist's lab. Similar studies exist for the other main streets of Halloween Town. The angular, expressionistic style that characterizes Halloween Town is accentuated in the overview of Town Square (right).

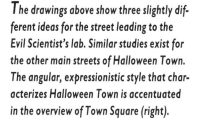

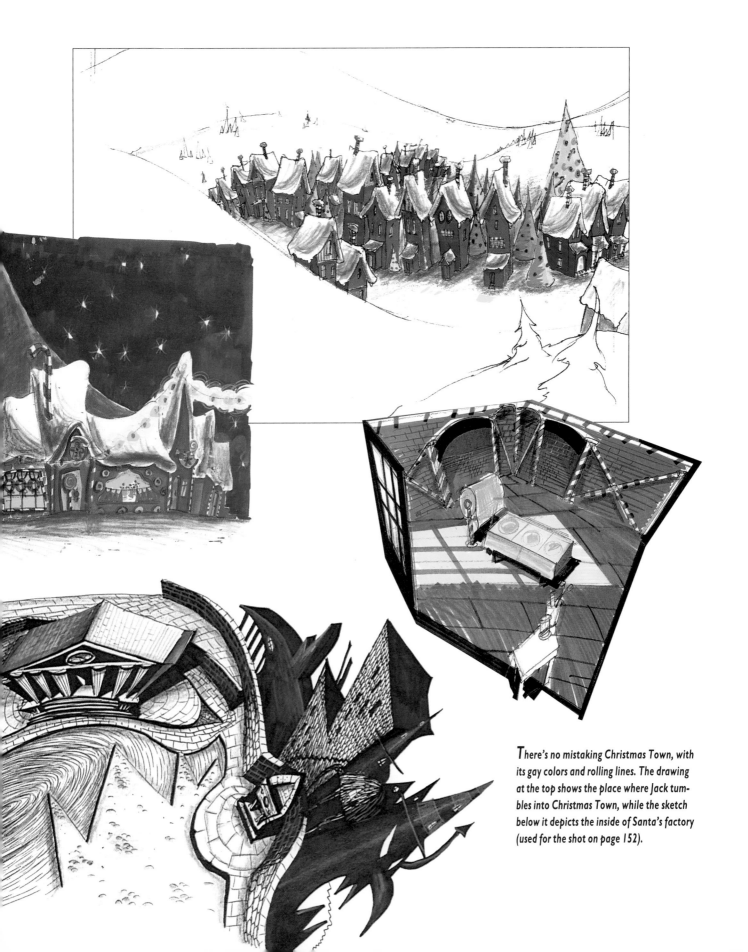

There's no mistaking Christmas Town, with its gay colors and rolling lines. The drawing at the top shows the place where Jack tumbles into Christmas Town, while the sketch below it depicts the inside of Santa's factory (used for the shot on page 152).

This weirdness is no accident. Taylor explains that by using isometric drawing pads in designing the Real World, the artists made sure that every object they drew lacked perspective. In contrast, Taylor points out, "Halloweenland has a totally bent perspective, and Christmas Town is kind of forced and squat." Because the artists were formal about the design approach, Taylor notes, "the Real World ended up looking weird by itself—quite disconcerting."

Boes feels that designing Oogie Boogie's lair was the weirdest experience. Selick wanted it to look one way under regular light and a different way under ultraviolet light. To accomplish this dual look, the artists conducted a series of tests, using mockups built by Boes and painting them with ultraviolet paints.

"In Oogie Boogie's lair, when the lights are on, you see all these torture devices, heavy steel and jagged edges," says Cronkhite. "But when the lights go off and the black light comes on, it's more naive, sort of

This preliminary drawing leads giddily in to the Halloweenland cemetery. The off-beat monuments jutting at odd angles contrast with the neatly rounded gravestones in the Real World cemetery (see page 19).

primitive, almost aboriginal." Asbury adds, "We studied cave paintings as inspiration."

Tim Burton's original drawings, as well as Rick Heinrichs's input, gave the art department the basic style and feeling for Halloweenland and Christmas Town, but they had to imagine the Real World and Oogie's lair from the ground up. Still, the odd rigidity of the Real World seems directly related to the bizarre suburban landscapes that have populated so many of Burton's films: Pee-wee's playhouse-gone-berserk in *Pee-wee's Big Adventure,* the gothic suburbia of *Frankenweenie,* the multihued cul-de-sac in *Edward Scissorhands.* In a way this is a tribute to these artists' ability to join fully in Burton's vision and enrich it. "Tim isn't around for all the nuts and bolts," comments Taylor, "but he's right in there in keeping an overall look, an overall feel. He's quite involved in the story, but with the day-to-day things, the hands-on stuff, he seems to be confident enough in what he's seen to let us go ahead."

*T*he art department showed Henry Selick dozens of ideas for Oogie's lair (bottom, far left) and his nightmarish torture devices (such as the sacrificial table below left). To make the task even more complicated, the artists had to figure out how each object's color would change in normal light and black, or ultraviolet, light—as suggested by the color studies for Oogie's roulette wheel (below) and the Iron Maiden (bottom).

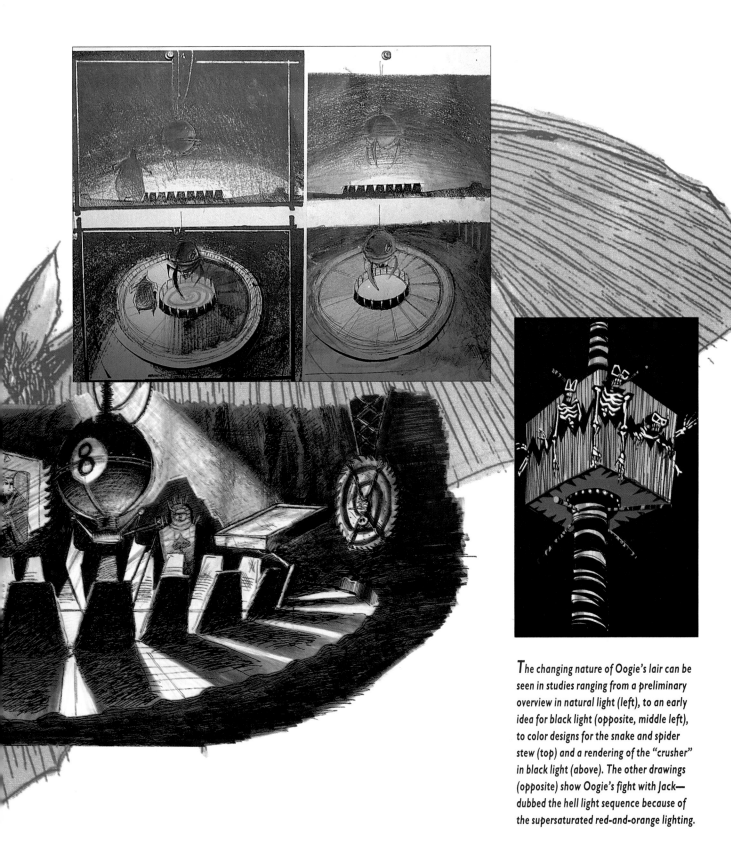

*T*he changing nature of Oogie's lair can be seen in studies ranging from a preliminary overview in natural light (left), to an early idea for black light (opposite, middle left), to color designs for the snake and spider stew (top) and a rendering of the "crusher" in black light (above). The other drawings (opposite) show Oogie's fight with Jack—dubbed the hell light sequence because of the supersaturated red-and-orange lighting.

After Tom Proost builds one of six copies of Oogie's roulette wheel (below), Stephanie Lesh paints it for use in normal light. Other wheels were coated with ultraviolet paint to turn fluorescent in black light. At right Todd Lookinland works on a large set of Halloween Town after receiving directions from Bo Henry (opposite, left). After the set is built, the surfaces are textured with Styrofoam and various plaster mixes.

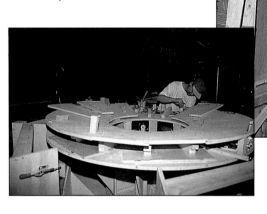

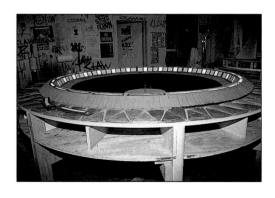

SET AND PROP DESIGN AND CONSTRUCTION

In the art department imagination soars. Within the confines of the story, and the directives of Tim Burton and Henry Selick, the artists are free to create whatever they want. And when they have conjured up a fantastical set, they send their vision down to Bo Henry, the set construction supervisor, and he gets it built.

Visit a live-action movie set and, chances are, everything will seem flimsy and temporary. Buildings that look perfectly solid on screen may be only thin fronts of plaster or canvas. The opposite is true on the *Nightmare* set—presenting a challenge to the set construction department.

"You build these incredibly detailed, highly sculptural, fanciful sets," Bo Henry says, "but underneath they're screwed and cross-braced and ugly—because the sets are literally abused and misused by animators and camerapeople." The sets have to be strong enough to hang lights on and to support the weight of animators, who may have to crawl onto a set to move the puppets. Moreover, every set has to be rock solid, because if anything were to jiggle, slip, move, or break, the shot would be lost. If the set doesn't hold up, Henry underlines, "it may be twelve or fourteen hours' work for the animator down the drain."

To the observer it seems surprising that in many instances this dauntingly high-tech work is done without intricate blueprints. Generally, Henry receives a drawing from the art department. After consulting with Selick and supervising animator Eric Leighton to find out precisely how the set will be used, set designer Gregg Olsson builds a model. Henry and Olsson determine where the camera needs to go, where the set

Even a relatively simple set, like the one for the Real World cemetery below, requires a sturdy, heavily braced wooden framework. The horizontal surface is equally solid, made of high-density particleboard, so the characters can be screwed tightly in place.

Models of Halloweenland (right and top) and the curling hill in its cemetery (above) guided set construction, as well as later detail drawings by the art department. Rick Heinrichs, who was instrumental in developing the look of Halloweenland, underlines a distinct advantage of creating sets for stop-motion animation: "You're free to design whatever you want without the limitations imposed by full size and live action."

can break apart for various camera angles within the shot, where lights have to hang, and where trap doors (for access) can be hidden.

"The camera is five or six times bigger than the characters," Henry points out, "so the set has to be built specifically to allow the camera to get into a position where it can read the images. In live action you can hide a light behind a column or place it overhead. Here, a light is bigger than the entire set, so we have to plan on that from the beginning."

Once Henry and Olsson have figured out the logistics, a detailed model and some relatively simple construction drawings are sent to the shop. The working drawings are little more than floor plans; the shop technicians pull most of the detail from Olsson's model and the art department's illustrations.

"This is a young crew," Henry says, "which is great since they don't have the normal expectations that a more senior crew might have. They don't ask, 'Where are the drawings?' They just take this stuff and build it without complaint. They can be relied on to be responsible for creating it out of their own heads, using just some fairly open-ended information."

In a project filled with challenges, Bo Henry remembers one set that seemed both unusual and impossible. Early in the film, when Jack Skellington is wandering in the forest, he discovers a group of "holiday" trees. He is drawn to one with a brightly colored Christmas tree door. As he reaches for the shiny doorknob, we see the forest behind him reflected in its surface. The doorknob and its reflection are on screen for only a second; few in the audience suspect how much labor was involved in attaining the shot.

"The crew had to work inside an eight-by-eight-by-eight-foot box for two weeks, creating a forced perspective image of what Jack sees in the

A drawing for a shot (like the one below of the Mayor announcing Jack's death) is translated into a small three-dimensional mock-up for the set builders to follow. Here the pen lines are important as a blueprint for getting texture to move through the set.

doorknob," says Henry. "We literally built a set to the view in the door-knob, then custom-built the set backward from that view."

Henry continues, "Some of the sets have been as large as forty by twenty feet. Others have been only a square foot. A lot of sets have been built for a single shot. If you broke it down to the labor of one person, it would be the equivalent of working for six months for a single eight-second shot."

While Henry and his crew build the actual sets, Mitch Romanauski and his staff of model makers create everything that turns the set into a living environment. They decorate the floors, walls, and trim. They also build everything that goes onto the set, from tables and chairs to more unusual things. "I had to make a tiny working doll," Romanauski remembers, "one of those dolls where when you raise it the eyes and mouth open. The whole doll, body and all, was an inch long. It had to work for a closeup, so it had to be perfect."

Romanauski and his crew have created thousands of props, some strikingly bizarre, some so normal that the eye barely registers that they aren't the real thing. Pointing to a still photograph of Santa Claus's living room, he explains, "The art department gave the drawing of this to us with the walls and partitions unfinished and just a few of the major furniture pieces roughed in. We put on the wallpaper and added the surface to the beams. We built the chair, made the carpet and made the wood flooring, created the pies, kitchen utensils, plants, and clock. We even made the long list that Santa's holding."

The props are made from a variety of materials, depending on how they will be used. The tiny pies stacked in Santa's kitchen are made of

Day after day Jeff Brewer and Pam Kibbee (below) arrange tiny cardboard houses for a view of the Real World from Jack's sleigh, while Tom Proost (bottom) constructs larger houses for Jack's jaunt from rooftop to rooftop. After the basic framework is made, details like shingles and strips of siding are glued to each house before painting begins.

*E*verything in the miniature world of stop-motion animation has to be constructed. A separate set, requiring weeks of work, was built for the reflected view in the doorknob (left), which appears for just seconds on screen. In transforming the drawing and model of Timmy's living room (middle) into a set, all the details, including the fire irons, had to be fabricated. And not only were the skeletal reindeer created, but also the Evil Scientist's plans for them (bottom).

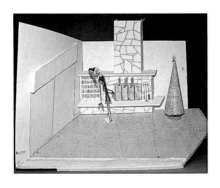

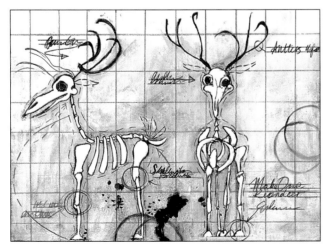

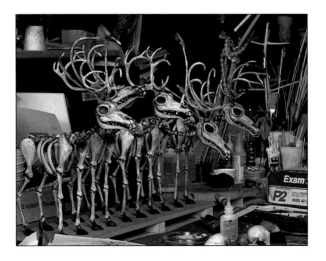

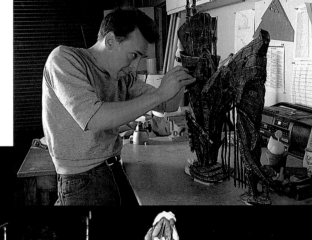

After turning a drawing of Oogie's Wheel of Misfortune into an actual object, Gretchen Scharfenberg checks its switchboard to make sure the tiny lights go on and off around the wheel (top). Fon Davis (above) follows an existing version of Jack's tower in constructing a new set. For the Halloween Town gate, Norm DeCarlo (above right) fashions a master sculpture, from which duplicates can be cast. On the set Scharfenberg (right) adds final touches to the snow-covered Halloweenland cemetery.

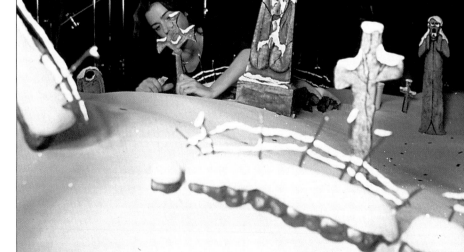

epoxy putty. To create pie pans in volume, one was molded in plastic, and the rest were vacuum-formed from this original. The crust was also sculpted from epoxy putty, then a mold was made so that multiples would be available.

Santa's long "naughty-or-nice" list looks like paper, but that would be impractical in stop-motion animation, where nothing can move even slightly between shots. Instead, Romanauski sandwiched a sheet of aluminum foil between two very thin sheets of paper. The list looks like paper, but it remains flexible and stays exactly where the animator wants it.

Again and again Romanauski is challenged by the task of making sure the props are both beautiful and durable. "A lot of the props are spidery, tall, thin kinds of things," Romanauski explains. "They're beautiful, but they may not be practical. We have to make sure they're animator-proof. If Santa is sitting on a chair with toothpick-sized legs, it's obviously not going to last very long."

Romanauski relishes some of the really odd props that *Nightmare* has given him the chance to make. "In one proposed scene, the Evil Scientist is disappointed in his creation, Sally," notes Romanauski. "He decides that he wants a new creation, one that works better. He uses a machine that's a kind of head selector. It's a spider machine with eight legs, and on the end of each one is a cup that holds a skull. It rotates and drops a skull into position. It's a weird rig."

While Romanauski and crew dress the sets, other details—particularly for exterior scenes—are provided by painter B. J. Fredrickson and her crew. "They are responsible for the textural finishes that are applied to these surfaces," Bo Henry explains. "For example, they have painted

The size of the set varies greatly depending on the shot. Animator Angie Glocka (top left) works on a shallow stage for the view of Santa ticking off names on his "naughty-or-nice" list (top right). For shots of Jack traveling in the sky, George Wong (above) works on a rigging system that will hold the sleigh steady yet allow it to be moved.

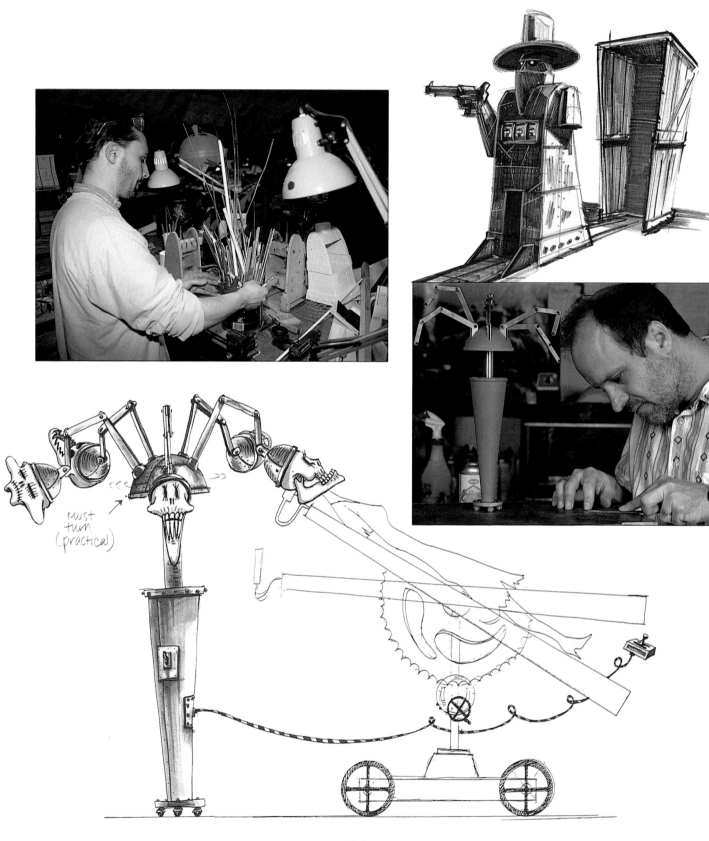

must
turn
(practical)

thousands and thousands of cobblestones, each of which first had to be sculpted by hand to give it a nice unique look before any paint went on."

Fredrickson is also in charge of painting the huge sky backdrops surrounding some of the sets. "Each particular world in this show has its own style," Fredrickson points out. "Halloweenland is black and white and gray with only occasional flashes of color. The skies are always gray and overcast, ominous, a bit reminiscent of Frankenstein movies. Christmas Town is bright and cheerful, very clean. For that I just painted flat skies, which were then lit with little star-shaped lights from behind. In the Real World the clouds are a lot more realistic and have more colors in them. But in the film what you see is the overcast night when Jack is delivering Christmas presents. It's a rainy, stormy sky, but—as opposed to the Halloween skies—there's more color in it, making it more real and also more dreary."

Fredrickson paints the backgrounds with a spray gun, a larger version of an airbrush, to give her skies what she describes as a "nebulous, distant look." She explains, "In live action my work is supposed to blend into the background and look real. But here it is actually supposed to look like a cartoon, like art."

All of *Nightmare's* world looks like art of the highest caliber. Despite the frustrations and tedium of this precision work, Romanauski says the experience has been unforgettable. "It's very hard work," he admits. "It's stressful and everyone gets burned out, but I think most people would agree with me that it's a once in a lifetime job. The Halloween stuff is so beautiful and fun to make. There have been many props that the model makers fought over for a chance to make. They were so eager to do it. That doesn't happen that often. It's happened a lot on this job."

Working from the art department's sketch, Marc Ribaud (opposite, left) improvises with different materials to fashion a one-armed bandit for Oogie's lair. Details are changed as the actual prop is built (the final version is on page 145). Mitch Romanauski (opposite, right) has to figure out how to make the artist's design for the Evil Scientist's skull machine function in three dimensions. B. J. Fredrickson (left) works on huge canvases, painting in the skies that surround many of the exterior sets.

*T*he armature for Santa's head has about fifty tiny parts that must be fitted together precisely (right) to give him a range of facial expressions, with eye, mouth, and even eyebrow movements. Before the full armature is assembled (below right), the joints are tightened and the head's fit is checked inside the foam face (below).

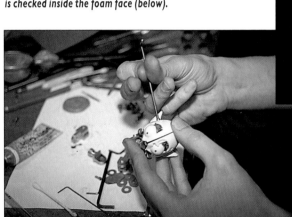

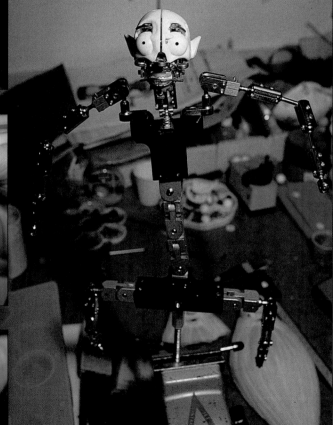

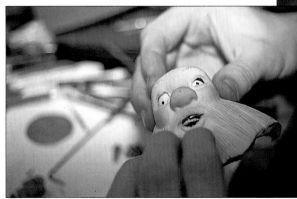

ARMATURES

Both stop-motion animation and conventional cel animation encourage the audience to believe that their characters are alive, but the difference is that in stop-motion the characters actually exist. They are physical, three-dimensional creatures who inhabit a solid universe.

While it would be pushing it to claim that the denizens of *Nightmare Before Christmas* are flesh-and-blood beings—Jack, after all, is mostly bones; Sally an animated rag doll; and Oogie Boogie, a huge burlap figure bulging with bugs—they do share one characteristic with you and me: they have a skeleton.

The skeletons for the stop-motion characters are called armatures. Armatures are usually made of aluminum and steel; sometimes they are augmented by wire or plastic. Although armatures are a part of the puppet that no audience member sees, they are in some ways the most important element in bringing Jack, Sally, and the rest of the icky gang to life.

According to John Reed, supervisor of mold making, in the earliest stages of design the challenge is to decide how a character will move. "We figure out the action that it needs," Reed explains. "Then we figure out what materials best give us that action. We also try to solve the other problems of animation, such as being able to move it smoothly from frame to frame and not have it 'pop'—that is, jump in fast movements that are not very well controlled. Having a good-quality armature is part of that."

"As soon as the character is designed, it comes to us," says armature

Merrick Cheney (below left) machines parts for an armature. Even a minor puppet like Howie (below) has a fairly complicated armature, requiring careful machining of dozens of small metal pieces.

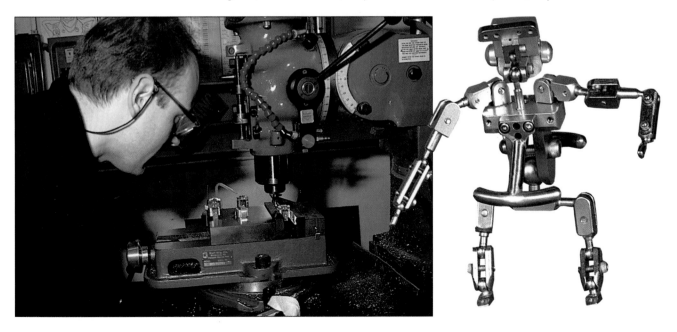

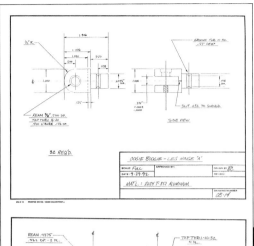

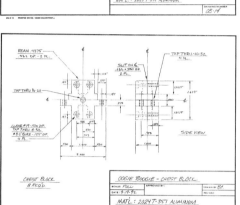

*T*o figure out the armature for Oogie Boogie, Blair Clark first traced the puppet's outline from a gridded photo of the sculpture (top right) and drew possible joints inside. Then he worked out detailed plans with accurate dimensions (above) for every part in Oogie's skeleton, so that exact multiples could easily be made. The 175 or so parts in this two-foot-high puppet must all be fitted together with screws and washers in the correct order (see photo at right).

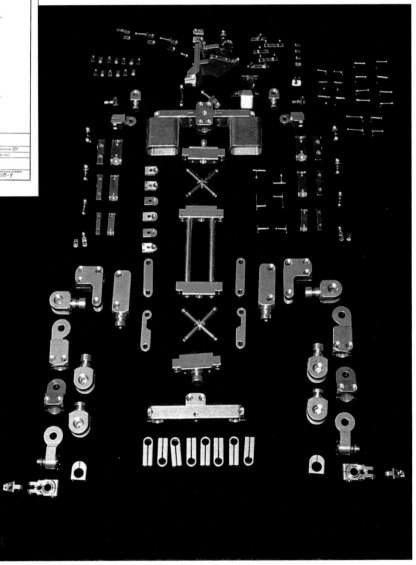

*B*lair Clark (above) begins assembling the armature for Oogie, which takes over a day to put together once all the parts are made. During assembly Chris Rand (top left) checks on the armature's alignment; later, animator Eric Leighton (top right) tests the armature's flexibility, tightening or loosening joints as needed. It is a feat of careful design that this six-pound armature can balance on one leg (see left).

NIGHTMARE BEFORE CHRISTMAS

maker Blair Clark. "The designers usually give us a sculpture or, better yet, a full-scale sketch of the front and side views. And they tell us what it has to do. There are a lot of characters in this show that have to do a lot of strange things."

The main requirement for an armature is that it must be able to hold whatever pose the character is put in without falling over or moving. In addition, every movement must be smooth, without any "pops," or sudden jumps. "You want to make the puppet as easy to animate as possible," indicates Clark.

After detailed blueprints are drawn up, the machine shop makes the joints and parts needed to build high-tech, movable skeletons. Multiple copies are made of some of the most-used joints so that the armature department can use them like incredibly intricate and expensive Tinkertoys. These joints are silver-soldered and chrome-plated. This step is necessary, explains Clark, because the armature is eventually covered with a readily oxidizing foam and the whole thing is baked in an oven. "The armature would rust if it wasn't plated," he says.

Most of the armatures were designed by Tom St. Amand—"the best in the business," according to Clark. St. Amand faced unusual challenges with the *Nightmare* armatures, especially in building Jack's skeleton. Director Henry Selick has nothing but praise for St. Amand's work: "He was able to make the smallest ankles, the smallest feet that were still able to support Jack's height. Any lesser armature maker would not have been able to pull it off; Jack would have been much thicker, much clunkier-looking."

Oogie Boogie presented almost the opposite type of challenge. "He's

The character design shows only the outside of a puppet like the Harlequin Demon (below). It is the armature maker who figures out how to make the head bobble on top of the mouth. When the armature is used, the joints gets loosened, so it is constantly sent back for retightening (below right).

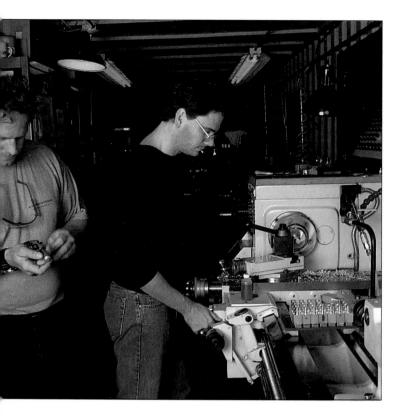

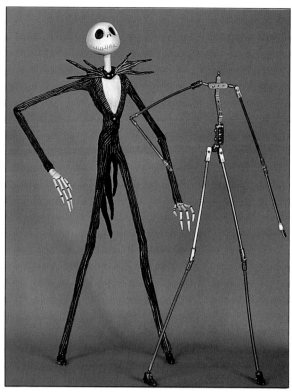

so big," exclaims Clark, "one of the biggest armatures I've ever seen." And big means strong. In the words of sculptor Norm DeCarlo, "You could tow a truck with Oogie's armature."

At the same time Oogie had to be able to slink and slide for his dance around Santa Claus. To get Oogie to undulate in this way, Clark made "pushers" (little metal rods with blunted ends).

Because of the methodical nature of stop-motion animation, the same character has to be on several stages at once. This means that duplicate armatures have to be constructed—often with minute differences. "We made a total of eight Jacks," says Clark. "Most were regular size, but Merrick Cheney, another armature maker, also built a half-scale size, which worked out well for a long shot."

During production, the armature department fluctuated in size. Its members—Clark, Cheney, St. Amand, Chris Rand, Eben Stromquist, Bart Trickel, and Lionel Orozco—not only built new armatures but also serviced those which were already in use. "Over a hundred armatures were made for this show," marvels Clark, not quite believing it himself. "I worked on *Robocop II* and we had nine armatures for the bad guy and four for Robocop and that was a big show. This is just insane!"

Chris Rand (top left) measures parts with a micrometer to find out exactly how much to machine off the metal, while Blair Clark turns the lathe. The armature for Jack (top right) is amazingly thin, and the puppet is not much thicker. Unlike Santa and Oogie, Jack does not have an armatured "skull"; instead, he has plastic replacement heads.

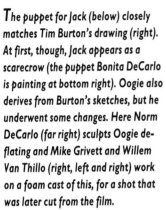

*T*he puppet for Jack (below) closely matches Tim Burton's drawing (right). At first, though, Jack appears as a scarecrow (the puppet Bonita DeCarlo is painting at bottom right). Oogie also derives from Burton's sketches, but he underwent some changes. Here Norm DeCarlo (far right) sculpts Oogie de-flating and Mike Grivett and Willem Van Thillo (right, left and right) work on a foam cast of this, for a shot that was later cut from the film.

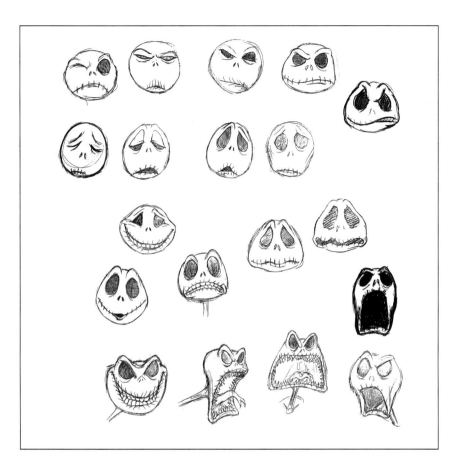

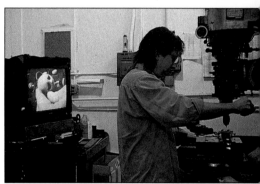

CHARACTER SCULPTING AND FABRICATION

The character department is the next logical step after armatures. They create the flesh that goes on the bones. But things are rarely that orderly on a stop-motion film. For John Reed, the mold-making supervisor, the ideal sequence would be for a puppet to be designed, the actions planned, and an armature made. The character would be sculpted over the armature, then molded, cast, and painted. The animator would animate it, the film would be developed, and the movie shown. "In reality," Reed admits, "it doesn't work that way at all. All these steps have to happen more or less simultaneously. If people don't communicate well with each other, then it's like the game of Chinese Whispers, where everybody interprets something differently all the way down the line."

For *Nightmare*'s character designers, the original inspiration and the biggest challenge came from the same source: Tim Burton. The drawings he had made at Disney were highly evocative: spooky, funny, creepy, weird —wondrously imaginative. But when it came to translating his drawings into real, three-dimensional characters, there was sometimes trouble.

Jack's expressions range from downcast to delighted to furious. To capture the variety of emotions in the drawing (top left), as well as the lip movements for his speaking and singing, Jack is outfitted with about 180 replaceable heads. Shelley Daniels (top right) sculpts the stitches and slight variations in one of the mouths. The process is repeated for each head, before multiples are cast. For Jack's appearance as Santa, Jeff Brewer (above) drills holes to hold the beard in the same place on all the heads.

"If you look at the original drawings of Jack Skellington by Tim Burton," says Eric Leighton, supervising animator, "Jack was twice as skinny as what we ended up shooting. We're at our limits: we've made him skinny, but we stopped where it was impossible."

Henry Selick remembers bargaining with Burton about the size of Sally's ankles. "We determined with her small feet and rather voluptuous body that she couldn't have the impossibly thin ankles Tim wanted. I came up with the idea that she'd wear socks, which would hide the ankles so the legs above could be thin. Tim agonized for a couple of days and finally said, 'Okay, if she has stripes on her socks, I can buy that.'"

That, in a nutshell, is the recurring problem for the *Nightmare* creators: balancing concept with execution and bringing a fanciful—impossible—sketch to animated life. The artists on the film see it is a challenge.

Taking the art department's concepts as a starting point, sculptors Shelley Daniels, Norm DeCarlo, Randy Dutra, and Greg Dykstra must find the right materials to make the puppet a reality. Their job is more than just copying the sketch. "I've been given a lot of latitude to interpret drawings," DeCarlo says. He points to a foam model of Oogie Boogie. "At one point," he comments, "Oogie was supposed to deflate, so we created a sculpture to test that. But he also had to twist, and the way he was designed made that impossible. So I had to change the 'sculpt'; it had to

Once a character design is approved by Selick, it is photocopied and several different color combinations are tried out, as with the Clown (below). The final color study, which Elise Robertson follows in painting the puppet (opposite), is on page 24.

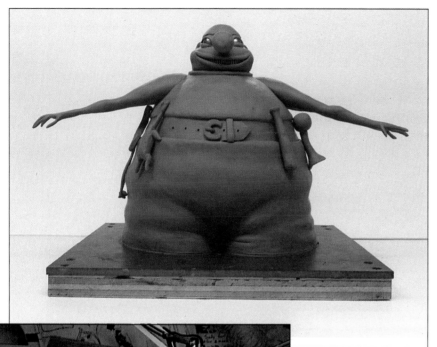

Working from the character design, the sculptor makes a clay model (like the early version of the Clown at left), which is used to make a mold for the puppet, allowing multiples to be cast. For the Evil Scientist, the color studies (below) were done for a standing figure, although the puppet was confined to a wheelchair.

*E*rik Jensen (right) whips up foam latex colored green for Oogie Boogie's skin in ultraviolet light. When the consistency is right, he adds a coagulant, and with Rob Ronning (far right), pours the mixture into a tube for injection into the mold (below). The foam settles in between an epoxy core and the mold itself. Ronning (below right) puts the mold into the oven, where it bakes for several hours to vulcanize the rubber. Ronning, Tony Preciado , and John Reed (bottom) are all needed to open the 200-pound mold.

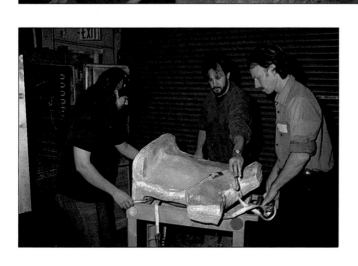

*A*fter carefully prying off the top of the mold (left), Ronning, Reed, and Preciado coat the foam with talcum powder (below) and then ease the cast out of the mold (below left). It is then brushed once more with powder to keep the latex from sticking to itself and put into the oven again for an hour or two to dry out.

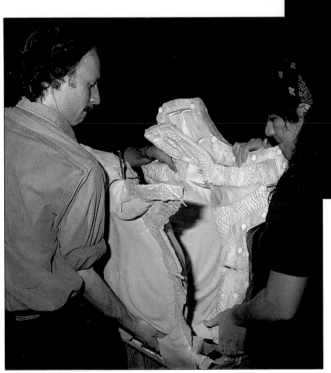

be molded and tested again before I could put all the texture on it. All this was very time-consuming" (and in the end the shot was cut from the film).

Once the characters have been sculpted, a mold is created so multiple puppets can be cast. The armature is placed in the mold and foam latex is injected, surrounding the armature and filling out the structure inside. The result is a replica of the character with a steel "skeleton" inside.

The puppet then moves up to the character fabrication department for its final grooming and dressing. The first step is to remove waste material left over from the casting process and correct imperfections in the foam surface. Called seaming, this requires laying a delicate patch of fine latex over the mold lines and any imperfections. The surface of each puppet is cleaned with alcohol to prepare it for painting. Some puppets are painted with a urethane-based paint that forms a flexible skin on the puppet. Others are treated with a rubber cement and solvent mixture that temporarily opens the surface of the foam, so the pigment adheres firmly.

"Our paints have to be very sturdy," emphasizes Bonita DeCarlo,

Sally's armature is put inside the mold (top left), so the foam latex covers it. Her hands (top right) are all cast separately, so they can easily be replaced. When the Sally puppet is first removed from the mold, there is a buildup of foam along the seams—called "flashing"—and this waste material has to be cut off (bottom left). The next step is to take wet latex and seal any imperfections, especially along the seams, as Lauren Vogt is doing with the Behemoth (bottom right).

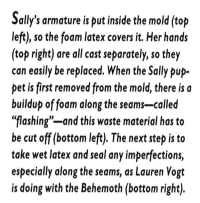

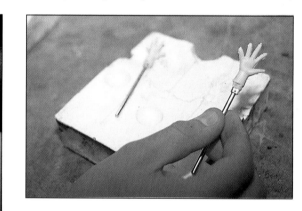

character fabrication supervisor. "The process of animation is very rough on the puppets, so the stronger we make the paint job, the better the puppets will hold up through a number of shots."

The fabricators also use a variety of materials when finishing the characters. They have a large selection of cloth fabrics, natural and synthetic furs, and fabric markers. "We also use pigmented powders," says DeCarlo, "to achieve the graphic look that *Nightmare* strives for."

Some of the *Nightmare* characters have their clothes merely painted on, but the major puppets have their own wardrobes. Yet nothing is precisely what it seems in this stop-motion world. Just because clothes look like they're made of cloth is no reason to assume they are.

Based on the color study (top left) and the "sculpt" (top right), the completed elf (bottom right) is one piece of foam latex (except for the legs), with a wire armature inside. Members of the fabrication department, including Mike Wick, Grace Murphy, and Facundo Rabaudi (bottom left, left to right), are constantly making new puppets and repairing old ones.

*F*ollowing the plan in front of her, Chrystene Ells (top) stuffs cotton balls into Oogie Boogie, providing padding between the armature and the skin. Later (above right), she adds shadows to Oogie's skin, as Liz Jennings works behind her. Using a needle, Jennings (above) pushes hair into the Wolfman (also called the Werewolf). Sally (right) has over 120 replacement faces.

"When it was decided that Sally needed a dress," Bonita DeCarlo mentions, "we had to plan out the stages of the creation of that dress very carefully. The first step was to have a dress sculpted for the puppet's body. That was then molded and cast in foam latex to provide a surface to lay the dress onto. The dress itself is made up of a silkscreened pattern that has been hand-painted, laid onto the foam, and carefully stitched."

Such incredible care is taken because of the nature of the Sally puppet and her movements. "When Sally walks or lifts her leg," DeCarlo says, "the dress moves with her. It even has a bit of memory. It remembers where it was and falls back into that place so the animator doesn't have to worry about it moving all over her body on the screen."

Hair presents a challenge. DeCarlo notes, "Sally's hair is made of foam latex that has been lined with lead so it can be animated precisely. Santa Claus, on the other hand, has a beard made with a wired foam core with fur laid on the top surface. For the Wolfman we used a technique called punching, which requires pushing individual hairs into the surface of the foam with a special needle device. We've used a number of different styles of hair in order to give each puppet a unique look."

While the armature lets a puppet's body and limbs be articulated for human—or inhuman—movements, its face is more difficult to animate. To give Jack and Sally a full range of expression, a series of replacement

T. Reid Norton paints the details on one of Sally's faces (top left), while Elise Robertson tightens a screw on the head that Sally's face pops onto (bottom left). Sally also has separate pupils and eyelashes that the animators can change to increase her range of expression. Using a toothpick, Mike Wick carefully glues strands of hair into Santa's beard (below).

heads was designed. Sally has ten different types of faces, and each type has eleven expressions. "They're like masks," says John Reed. "Her eyes can always be looking in the same direction from frame to frame, but you can pop her face off. There are also lip-synching mouths within each expression so she can enunciate everything she needs to say."

Faces aren't the puppets' only replaceable parts. Bonita DeCarlo indicates, "We keep a ready supply of hands, shoes, even extra castings of arms, which can be quickly exchanged for damaged or broken pieces. We also have replacement eyelids with delicate lashes. We have thousands of those. One person spends a lot of time making sure we never run low."

Fabricating the puppets is only half the job. After each character has finished a shot, it is returned to fabrication to be cleaned. Armatures break, replacement faces chip, foam wears out (particularly around the joints), and fabric tears. Light-colored puppets like Sally or the Evil Scientist get dirty quickly and can be used only for a shot or two before they must be returned to the mold department for recasting.

"There are approximately sixty puppets on the sets every week," notes DeCarlo. "We have to maintain those while prepping the next sixty that will be up the next week. There are 227 puppets in this film. That's a lot of puppets."

*T*o repair a hole in the Evil Scientist's mouth (below), Lauren Vogt improvises, using glue and latex—whatever works. In the storeroom, which is filled with puppets taking a rest in between performances, Tim Burton (right) poses with the stars of the show—Jack and Sally.

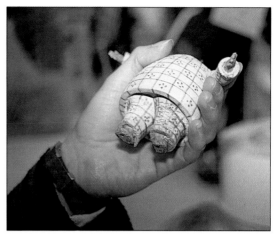

Most of the lead characters have a variety of replaceable parts. In the storeroom, for example, there are bins stuffed with heads and mouths for Barrel and Shock (top left). Jack's heads (left) are kept in boxes in numbered order to coordinate with the lip-synch script (see page 159). Sally's eyelids and lashes (above) constantly have to be recast and individually painted. On stage the puppets often get dirty and are sent back to fabrication to be cleaned (top right).

Angie Glocka and Jim Aupperle (right) work on the shot of Timmy careening down the stairs (below) to greet Santa (see page 64). In animating Timmy, Glocka tried to make him move like a kid pretending to be an airplane. For Aupperle, the challenge was to position the camera correctly at the one angle that worked with the isometric perspective used for the set.

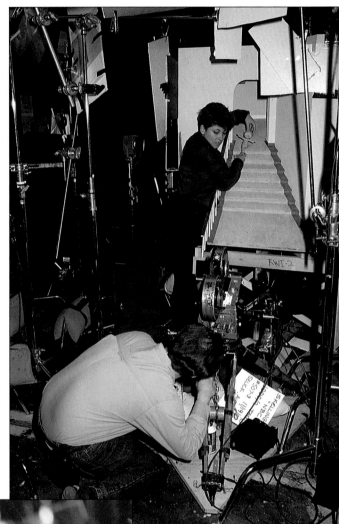

ANIMATION AND CAMERAWORK

All the work of creating storyboards and sketches and designing sets and characters leads to the cramped, underlit cubicles that serve as animation stages. While all the departments continue to have input, the animation itself is an almost solitary act: one animator, one camera, one scene.

You can watch a stop-motion animator at work for an hour or a day and never notice the slightest progress. Every new position the puppet is placed in is so like the one before that the sequence barely registers to the human eye. Stop-motion animators are miracle workers: technicians, artists, actors, engineers, all rolled into one. They have to bring originality and ingenuity to their work but at the same time make sure that their animation of a character melds perfectly with everyone else's.

Many different animators worked with Jack Skellington. For example, Loyd Price did an early scene where Jack tosses a coin to some musicians, while Tim Hittle animated most of Jack's next appearance, when he sings his lament. Yet in the final film, Jack appears as a single personality. "Every character has its own unique repertoire that each animator

The storyboard (below) guides Owen Klatte (opposite, bottom) as he animates the sequence in which Jack instructs Lock, Shock, and Barrel to kidnap Sandy Claws. But, as Klatte explains, while working on a shot, the animator fleshes out the storyboard, often "adding gags to make it fun."

Oogie's lair is seen from different angles in both normal and black (ultraviolet) light. Before animating Oogie for the camera, Eric Leighton (above and right) rehearses the puppet's dance. He even tries out the steps himself to get a feel for how the body should move. On another set (opposite bottom), Owen Klatte animates Oogie's taunting of Santa under ultraviolet light. And on yet another stage (opposite, top), Rich Lehmann checks the camera angle, while Aaron Kohr wires some lights for a shot of Jack and Oogie's fight.

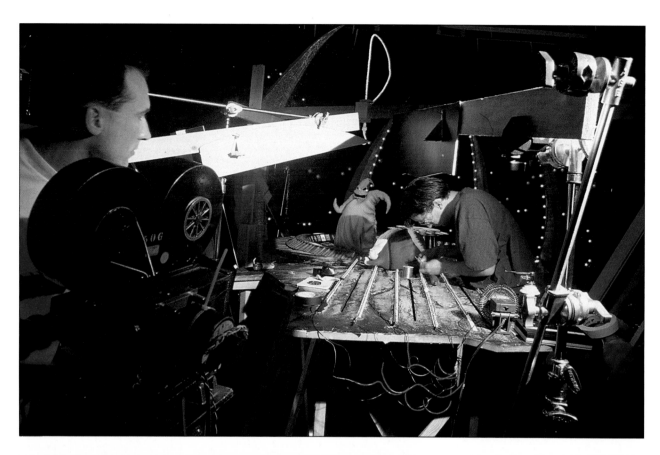

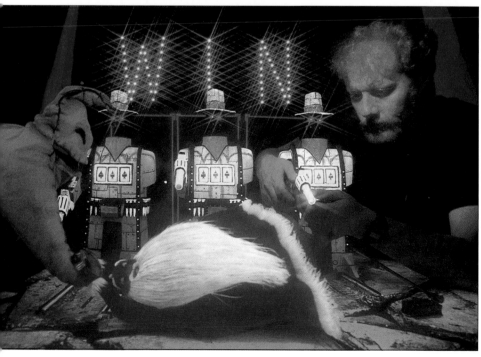

has to be able to duplicate," stresses supervising animator Eric Leighton. "Not only must they all perform it, but they must make it believable that it's the same guy throughout, regardless of their personal styles."

Each animator is an actor who creates a performance through a puppet. But it is one thing to find the perfect gesture to define a character, and quite another to break that gesture down into microseconds and spend a week bringing it to life. Each second of action must be broken down into twenty-four distinct motions—a task that sounds immeasurably easier than it really is.

"It's something that has to be acquired," indicates animator Angie Glocka. "Something happens where you start looking at time in a different way. You automatically start breaking action down in a slower time frame. It's like acting but in slow motion. You get into a rhythm and are kind of performing it but very slowly. Concentration is really important."

To get an idea of just how important concentration is, consider this: at the end of production there were nineteen stages and fourteen animators working simultaneously. Yet their combined efforts produced about only seventy seconds of finished film per week.

Leighton notes, "On a standard Disney animated feature, the average shot length is about four seconds. On this show, the average shot is

Henry Selick (below) shows Paul Berry one idea for the dance Jack does as a scarecrow at the beginning of the film, and Berry tries this out with the puppet on the set (right). Berry also studied the scarecrow's movement in The Wizard of Oz, *and he asked Beth Schneider, a production assistant with dance training, to perform some steps.*

five and a half to six seconds. We have even done ten-, fifteen-, twenty-second shots on *Nightmare Before Christmas,* which is a pretty risky thing to do in stop-motion. We've put as many as ten or eleven days into shooting a single shot."

Animator Owen Klatte points out, "It's very common these days in animation—especially because of MTV—to make things very quick and fast. But Henry Selick wanted to get more of a feeling of a live-action musical into this film, to get long, elegant shots into it."

Nightmare demands longer shots because the camera is always on the move. The film is filled with crane shots, tracking shots, camerawork of the most dazzling kind. In a live-action film, the camera is placed on a crane or a "truck" and moved with the action. But when the actors move about in twenty-fourth-of-a-second increments, filming them with fluid camera movement is problematic. That's where computers come in.

The motion control ("mocon") camera is a distant cousin of the industrial robot that revolutionized the auto industry. The length of the shot and direction and speed of the camera movement are programmed into a computer, so every time a frame of film is exposed, the camera moves an infinitesimal degree. "Programming the mocon is an interesting synthesis between left brain and right brain," claims director of photography

In animating some of the characters for a shot of "Making Christmas," Kim Blanchette has to lie down on stage at times simply to reach them. He doesn't do this just once; he has to climb back up and move them again for each frame on a twelve-day-long shot.

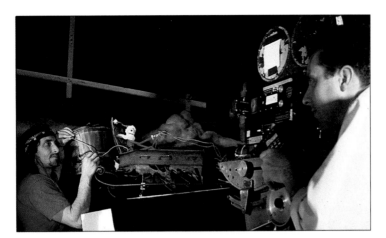

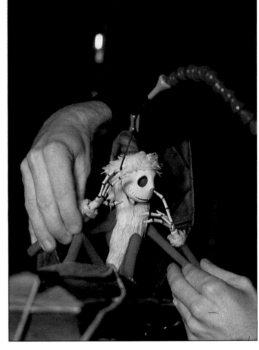

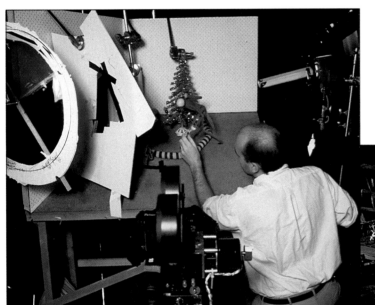

On screen Jack appears as one character, but in reality several Jacks are filmed on different stages. For example, Justin Kohn (top left) animates Jack driving his sleigh, as Matt White checks the camera framing, while on another stage (top right) Joel Fletcher animates a duplicate Santa Jack. Steve Buckley (above) works on a Christmas Eve scene. And another stage (right) is set up for Jack's takeoff in his sleigh from Halloween Town.

Pete Kozachik. "You have to know what the bits and bytes are doing, but you also have to have a feel for the quality of the shot. The mocon is used to enhance the image rather than impress with technical acumen."

Some camera movement, however, is still done the old-fashioned way. When the length of the shot has been determined, the number of frames to be exposed is figured out and a long piece of tape is placed along the route of the camera movement. A mark is made on the tape, and as each frame is exposed, the camera is moved forward one notch. "It's a bit more limiting," says Kozachik. "You can't be quite as sculptural or as specific about the feel of the camera movement."

The tape method is used mainly for camera pans or tilts. "When we get into a major flying camera move," Kozachik notes, "it's really a lot more expeditious to let the robot do it. It's just not as likely to screw up."

One reason each shot takes so long to complete on this film is that the animators make extensive tests before shooting the "hero" shot (the actual take). "We may shoot four or five tests on a shot," Eric Leighton indicates. "We wait until the camera crew's done with the lighting for the day, and if we have an hour we'll shoot a fast test on tens or twenties."

*Anthony Scott (below) adjusts Jack's position after he has fallen into the arms of an angel in the Real World cemetery (see the set at left and storyboard for the song "Poor Jack" on bottom). **This complicated sequence took months to complete (as Scott describes on page 153).***

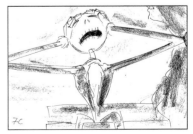

In animating the scene where Jack asks Sally to sew his Santa outfit (above left and right), Owen Klatte tries to convey, through the puppets' gestures, the miscommunication between the two. To make the animation look smooth from frame to frame, without any "pops" or sudden jumps, Klatte refers to a video screen (at far left above), which shows the previous frame.

Shooting on "tens or twenties" means that each major pose of the puppet is held for ten or twenty frames—what the animators call a "pop through." The idea is to test out the blocking of the scene, check out the lighting, and anticipate problems for the hero shot, which is "shot on ones," with one movement for each frame of film exposed.

"Since we're not doing a cel-animated film," stresses Leighton, "we can't go back and correct a drawing. We start on frame one and end up at the end of the shot. We can only go through it forward. You just don't know what you're going to run into until you've worked your way through the shot a few times."

Most of the animators agree that the extensive testing is one of the best things about working on the film. It is one of the elements that makes *Tim Burton's Nightmare Before Christmas* a masterpiece of stop-motion animation.

"I've never been allowed to do tests like I do here," says animator Anthony Scott. "Usually they give you your bit and say, 'Just go for it. Do your best.' And there's no time to go back and reshoot or test things you're not sure about. This project gives us the freedom to do that."

Once the hero shot is underway, most animators use a frame storage device with a video screen to help keep track of things. "With this system," explains Owen Klatte, "I can flip between the previous two frames I shot and the current frame I'm working on. I can check how far a character moves in a couple of frames and make sure everything's moving in the right direction. Sometimes I draw lines directly on the video screen, an outline of the character, so I can see over a course of, say, twenty frames, how the increments have changed."

A particularly tricky problem on this project is making sure that one scene flows easily into the next. Animator Mike Belzer points out, "If you see Jack walking out of a door and in the next scene he's walking through the woods, those might be shot six months apart because those are two totally different sets."

Other sequences are problematic because they are animated by two animators at once. Belzer recalls, "There's a two-and-a-half minute scene when Jack sings 'Jack's Obsession.' It might take one animator six months to do that. So we had two identical sets built and used two Jack puppets. Angie Glocka animated the first half of the song, and I animated the second half. But it appears to be one continuous sequence in the film."

The sequence in which Jack awakens in a cemetery after being shot down and sings "Poor Jack" was animated entirely by Anthony Scott (ex-

Pat Sweeney peers through the camera to check the scene where Jack returns to Halloween Town in a snowmobile after discovering Christmas. He not only makes sure the framing is right, but also looks for any necessary changes in lighting or adjustments to the set, such as touching up the paint on a particular building.

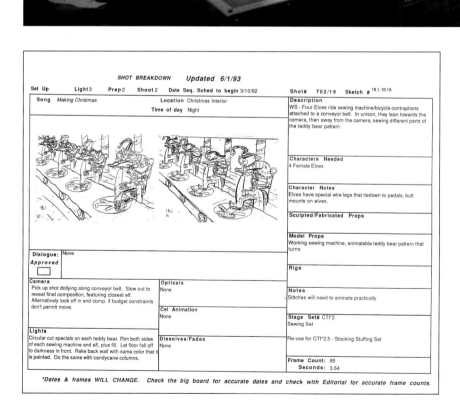

*E*ven a brief shot in the film, such as the elves sewing teddy-bear patterns during "Making Christmas" (right), requires a lot of work from every department. A sketch (above) shows the basic staging of the shot, while the shot breakdown sheet (below right) includes the storyboard script and details all the elements needed, from props to lighting. In this case, a change was made, and only three elves, rather than four, were used in the actual shot.

SHOT BREAKDOWN   **Updated** 6/1/93

Set Up	Light 3	Prep 2	Shoot 2	Date Seq. Sched to begin 3/10/92	Shot# 702/19 Sketch # 18.1, 18.1A

Song *Making Christmas*   **Location** Christmas Interior   **Time of day** Night

Description
WS - Four Elves ride sewing machine/bicycle contraptions attached to a conveyor belt. In unison, they lean towards the camera, then away from the camera, sewing different parts of the teddy bear pattern.

Characters Needed
4 Female Elves

Character Notes
Elves have special wire legs that tiedown to pedals, butt mounts on elves.

Sculpted/Fabricated Props

Model Props
Working sewing machine, animatable teddy bear pattern that turns

Dialogue: None
Approved ☐

Rigs

Camera
Pick up shot dollying along conveyor belt. Slow out to reveal final composition, featuring closest elf.
Alternatively lock off in end comp. if budget constraints don't permit move.

Opticals
None

Cel Animation
None

Notes
Stitches will need to animate practically

Stage Set# CTI*2
Sewing Set

Re-use for CTI*2.5 - Stocking Stuffing Set

Lights
Circular cut specials on each teddy bear. Rim both sides of each sewing machine and elf, plus fill. Let floor fall off to darkness in front. Rake back wall with same color that it is painted. Do the same with candycane columns.

Dissolves/Fades
None

Frame Count: 85
Seconds: 3.54

Dates & frames WILL CHANGE. Check the big board for accurate dates and check with Editorial for accurate frame counts.

cept for some Zero shots, which Richard Zimmerman animated). Although it's only about three minutes long, it took months to complete. "I began work on it in October 1992 and continued through the end of March 1993," Scott says.

In this scene, the only characters are Jack and his ghost dog Zero. To make Zero look transparent, he is sometimes double-exposed onto the film, sometimes an optical element, and sometimes projected into the shot with a "beam splitter," a two-way mirror that is set in front of the camera lens at a forty-five-degree angle. With the beam splitter, Zero is animated away from the main set and shot against a black background, so that he appears transparent when his image is mixed into the scene.

Confusing? It gets worse. While animating a scene with Zero and Jack, Scott found out just how dumbfounding the experience could be. "Because we were using the beam splitter," Scott recalls, "I had to animate Zero on the blacked-out set and Jack on the cemetery set. Zero was actually several feet away, but through the camera he appeared in the cemetery. We had a video monitor right next to the camera so I could match the characters' eye lines. It's real important to me that the characters relate well."

"At one point," Scott continues, "Jack grabs a hat out of the dog's mouth. Now the dog is transparent and the hat is real, and there's a frame where the hat has to switch over from Zero's mouth into Jack's hand. That was the toughest shot I've done. It took five days. Five long days."

Anything can change once the first tests of a shot are reviewed. After the filming of Santa reading his list got underway (below), it was decided that Mrs. Claus (who is only glimpsed in the background) looked too elf-like. Fabrication was called in to snip away and change the shape of the puppet.

*P*aul Berry recalls the fun of animating Jack during "The Town Meeting Song" (right)— of creating a performance for "a character who is also putting on a show." But "when Jack turns away from the audience and lets the pretense drop, you see the real Jack," Berry notes (see the stage below right). At first the crowd shots were animated by Angie Glocka and Steve Buckley on another stage, but at the end the two sets were brought together (below).

Nightmare's weird characters offered many challenges to the animators. Trey Thomas describes the huge Oogie Boogie, for example, as "like no other puppet I have ever worked with." Yet one character everybody thought would be trouble was anything but: Jack Skellington. A typical stop-motion puppet is short and squat with extra-large feet for easy balance. Jack is impossibly tall and thin, with tiny feet, thin ankles, and outrageously long arms. A puppet, in short, to give any animator pause.

Owen Klatte reflects, "Jack is definitely not as bad as I thought he was going to be. He's very tall and you have certain problems with him, but overall he has a lot of movement, a lot of freedom."

"You almost get spoiled when you play with a puppet as nice as Jack Skellington," claims Mike Belzer. "He is this beautiful, thin armature that has virtually no foam binding."

"He's the easiest puppet in the world," agrees Angie Glocka. "He's like a walking armature. He's the best, most fun character, which is really lucky for us because he's the star of the show."

To make sure Jack and everything else look just right, the animators and camera crew constantly review their shots with Selick and Stan Webb,

Mike Johnson (left) helps set up the shot that leads into "Sally's Song," as Justin Kohn (right) reaches in to animate Sally. When she walks through the crowd in this scene, Sally is on a model mover (a mechanical device that moves the puppet). For her actual song, Sally is animated on a different set by Trey Thomas, who tries to make her movements fit the charm and innocence of Catherine O'Hara's singing voice.

Camera assistant Carl Miller looks through the lens as Ken Willard, Mike Johnson, and Richard Zimmerman (left to right) prepare the puppets for a shot of Town Square involving over fifty characters. In the foreground is the arm of the motion control camera, or mocon, which uses a computer to control the camera movement.

the film's editor. Each morning Webb cuts the previous day's footage into the "rough cut" of the film, replacing earlier shots or storyboards, so the new take can be seen in context, with what comes before and after.

Although every scene is carefully storyboarded beforehand, there are still changes once shooting begins. "The timing may not be right," notes Webb, "or something may not be clear." One example he gives is the scene where Sally picks up a bottle of fog juice: "We thought in the storyboard that was just one shot. But once we filmed it, it was hard to read. We used a long shot and cut to a closeup of the bottle, so you can read the words 'fog juice.' But mostly it's the other way; usually we over-storyboard and then find we need less animation to make the point."

For everyone involved at the filming stage, the process is one of constant testing and readjustment to make everything come together.

*E*die Ichioka looks over Andrea Biklian's shoulder (top) in the editing room, as they examine the film using a synchronizer. One of the most important editing tools is the flatbed (above left), which allows the picture and soundtrack to be viewed together. Production staff members like George Young and Alia Agha (above) are constantly consulting the "big board," which shows the entire production schedule, day by day, stage by stage, shot by shot. On stage, Pete Kozachik, Loyd Price, Jim Aupperle, and Brian Van't Hul (left, left to right) confer on a shot of the musicians in Halloween Town.

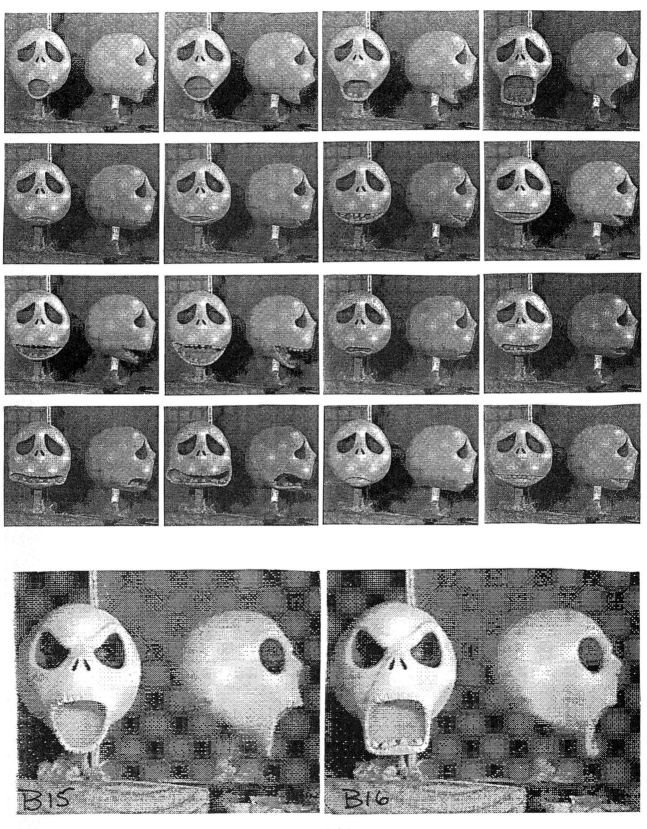

Dan Mason (left) uses a computer to develop a lip-synch "script" for puppets with replacement heads like Jack. "To create a menu of different heads, so I can choose which head is appropriate with which sound," Mason explains, "I took a video camera and shot a frame of each head and scanned the images into the computer" (part of the menu for Jack is shown opposite). After breaking down the character's speech phonetically and selecting appropriate heads, Mason runs the whole sequence through on the computer to see if it works.

ADDING SOUND AND SCORING

Creating the soundtrack for *Nightmare Before Christmas* and blending it with the film was a complicated process. To make the puppets seem to actually speak and sing, all the dialogue had to be recorded before filming began. This was especially important for Jack and Sally, who had numerous replacement heads, each with the mouth articulating a different sound. The animators had to know which head to use for each frame.

Here the computer helped. Dan Mason, the track reader, analyzed every frame of a character's speech on the soundtrack and matched it with a picture of the puppet's head from a menu of possibilties on his computer. He then printed out a "head" script for the animators.

During filming, the script continued to evolve, so sometimes dialogue had to be rerecorded later. Or there might be changes in a character's style. Chris Lebenzon, who helped with sound dubbing, cites Jack's speaking voice, some of which was rerecorded to make Jack livelier.

Finishing the music was one of the last stages of film production. Although music editor Bob Badami created a temporary soundtrack for screening purposes, Danny Elfman could not compose the actual musical score, the "incidental" or "background" music, until the very end.

Usually the composer receives a black-and-white pencil version of an animated film, so the score can be composed while the animation is in the works. But in stop-motion animation, Elfman explains, "There's either finished footage or there's no footage. There's no temporary footage, no black-and-white version that is busily being colored in. As a result, I couldn't score the movie until all the animation was done."

Although it was an "intense pressure" job, Elfman had a head start. He had already composed some thirty minutes of songs for the seventy-minute movie, cutting his job almost in half. Moreover, the main musical themes already existed in song form, so he could adapt those themes to the dramatic needs of the underscore. "There was so much thematic material already there," he recalls, "that creating significant new thematic material would have been a detriment to the film. The main problem was choosing which material I wanted to rely on most heavily for the score."

Many of Elfman's most beautiful and powerful scores were composed for and recorded by huge orchestras with nearly 100 instruments. The dark grandeur of *Batman* (1989), the melancholy loveliness of *Edward Scissorhands* (1990), and the Gershwinesque lushness of *Dick Tracy* (1990)—all Elfman scores—recall the majesty of the great film composers of the past he most admires: Bernard Herrmann, Alfred Newman, and Miklos Rozsa. The score for *Nightmare,* however, is smaller and more eccentric, using a mid-sized orchestra of fifty to sixty pieces. "I wanted a very punchy, old-fashioned sound on this," Elfman says. "I wanted it to sound (even though it's in stereo) as if it were recorded in 1951."

While working with the orchestra, Bob Badami notes, it was important to keep the music in close synch with the picture. So a computer was used to develop a sophisticated metronome the musicians could follow, creating the illusion that the sound and images were made together.

Although there are many choices on the computer menu for Sally's head (a few of which are shown below), Dan Mason tried to keep the total number to a minimum, deciding on ten or eleven essential mouth shapes for each of her expressions.

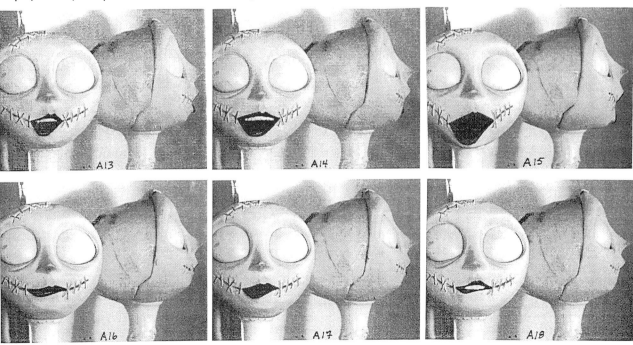

For one effects animation idea, Mike Cachuela (left) sketches Oogie's shadow, so it can seem to loom over some dice in a quick glimpse of his lair at the end of Lock, Shock, and Barrel's "Scheming Song."

POSTPRODUCTION

On a normal live-action film, the end of shooting is only the beginning of a long postproduction process that includes editing, music scoring, sound effects, special effects, and looping (rerecording of dialogue). Editing is a particularly important part of live-action postproduction; scenes are often filmed from a variety of angles or with different emphases and then the best take is chosen afterward.

In animation, however, the process is different. It is far too expensive and time-consuming to film a scene more than once in order to select a good take. So meticulous preplanning has to take the place of "fixing it in editing." Much of this preplanning occurs in the storyboard stage. The storyboard artists sketch different versions of scenes for the animators and director, allowing them to "edit" the film before any actual footage is shot. As a result, the editing process on *Nightmare Before Christmas* consists mostly of joining completed scenes together and, on occasion, optically "erasing" a light or cable that was impossible to keep out of the scene.

The postproduction process also involves the addition of effects animation that cannot be done until the stop-motion footage is completed. Using traditonal cel animation techniques, storyboard artist Mike Cachuela animated a few two-dimensional images like ghosts and shadows. Effects animator Gordon Baker also provided conventional animation, using paper as well as cels. For example, when the Evil

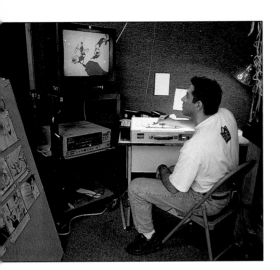

Scientist brings the reindeer skeletons to life, Baker animated the electricity coming out of the electrodes, "zapping the reindeer into life."

For these kinds of effects, the drawn animation has to interact with the stop-motion, which requires turning the three-dimensional puppets into drawings. "I have to wait until they're finished shooting their puppet animation," Baker explains. "Then I get a work print from them, which has to be projected onto an animation stand and rotoscoped—traced, frame by frame—so I can animate around the character."

Effects animation is added to the stop-motion footage in a variety of ways. Sometimes an effect is drawn before the stop-motion is begun. The drawing is then projected directly onto the set. "They shoot the puppet doing its action," Baker says, "then they back-wind the film and set up a card and project my animation onto the same set and double-expose it that way."

At other times the effects are combined with the animation during the postproduction process. For example, after Baker drew a series of snowflakes in black ink on white paper, they were photographed in negative and combined with the scene, where the snowflakes are seen as white. "I've done snowflakes, steam, some fire effects, radio waves that emanate from a tower," Baker notes. "Most of the things I've done are in black-and-white; then they add color later with gels or an optical process."

The effects animators' work is not meant to be noticed by the audience. Take the dramatic sequence in which Jack, dressed as a scarecrow,

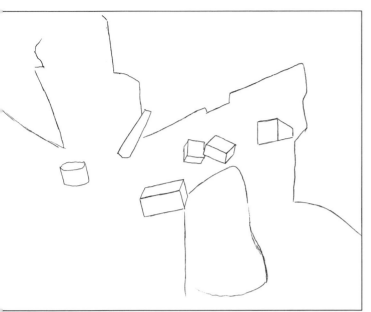

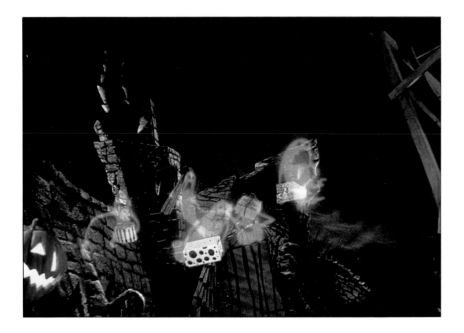

Gordon Baker (opposite, left) looks at a rough video test of effects animation of some ghosts carrying packages. To create the ghosts, the effects animators first took the work print of a frame (opposite, right) and traced the outlines of the packages and other elements they needed to consider (top left). After sketching the ghosts in pencil (top right), they inked them in (above), creating a cel. They did this for each frame in the shot, before checking the results on video. In the final print of the film (left), the two-dimensional ghosts blend in with the three-dimensional set.

catches fire. Here the three-dimensional and two-dimensional elements blend seamlessly. The part where Jack lights the torch was filmed with real flames. But when he brings the torch to his mouth, effects animation came into play. The flames that dance across his body as he somersaults into the fountain are drawings added to the picture in postproduction. Yet, because everything else is three-dimensional, the flames seem equally real. That is the power of this kind of effects animation.

The efforts of many hands come together in the final film. And in the movie theater, when Jack disappears down a chimney (right), Lock, Shock, and Barrel set off in their walking tub (below), the Easter Bunny and the Behemoth stare in mutual surprise (opposite, right), or Sally picks a flower outside the gates of Jack's house (opposite, bottom), the audience is left with the magical sense of a make-believe world that somehow really exists.

THE FINISHED PRODUCT

Nightmare Before Christmas took well over a decade to grow from Tim Burton's original poem and sketches to the groundbreaking feature film. But for everyone who had a hand in its production, the wait was definitely worthwhile.

"It's a very rich film," emphasizes sculptor Norm DeCarlo, "there's so much going on. Tim and Henry not only asked for but demanded a high level of acuity in detail and design. Working on this picture has been nothing but fun. There's nothing better than to be able to stretch your imagination and challenge your abilities."

Animator Angie Glocka adds, "I think people will really like this movie, particularly if they are Tim Burton fans. It's a really sweet film. It looks a little scary, but it isn't forbidding. I think it's a good kid's film. But it's a good grown-up film, too."

For Tim Burton, this film represents the satisfaction of realizing a dream that has occupied him for a third of his life. "You have to care about everything you do," he says, "but this film is special for me. The characters are very personal to me. Sometimes you're sitting there drawing and you don't even know what you're doing; it comes straight from your subconscious. This film has all the elements I wanted for it: the holidays (I love both Halloween and Christmas), beautiful but misunderstood characters, drama, sadness, optimism. When I watch it now, after having had it in me for so long," he sighs deeply, "I love it."

The Vision

*T*im Burton likes to explore new ways of looking at things—for example, taking giant Polaroids of his puppets (right). At Tim Burton Productions, he and his energetic production executives, Jill Jacobs and Diane Minter, are involved in developing new projects, publishing, and merchandising. His drawings, such as his early sketches of Barrel and Shock (below) and a rendering of Jack welcoming Santa's gift of snow (below right), are always crucial to his vision.

TIM BURTON

Tim Burton's Nightmare Before Christmas represents an unusual collaboration. It definitely reflects Burton's initial vision and shows the mark of his hand. At the same time it owes much of its impact to its director, Henry Selick.

The two men first formed a bond out of their frustration while working at Disney Studios in the early eighties. "Neither Henry nor I was really in our element at Disney," Burton says. "I did some design work for *The Black Cauldron* (1985) that never got used and worked on about ten projects that never got off the ground. Henry was also working on a lot of projects that never got made. He couldn't take it there anymore. So we struck up a friendship." Burton laughs, "A 'Where the hell are we?' sort of thing."

"In the art and film world," Selick explains, "you find out that there are five people out there who are very much like yourself, and you're either going to work well together or hate each other and be jealous of one another. Fortunately, Tim Burton and I get along well; we share a lot of common interests. We live on the same planet—if not in the same neighborhood—in our sensibilities."

Although little of Burton's early work made it into Disney feature films, he did make two short films at the studio that expressed his unique point of view. The first, *Vincent* (1982), is a stop-motion film about a little boy (who strongly resembles Burton) who is obsessed with horror stories. *Vincent* is narrated by Burton's hero, Vincent Price.

"It was a weird time at Disney, and some things slipped through the cracks," Burton notes. "I think *Vincent* was just something they let slide."

Burton admits that "it was nice for a couple of years to just sit in a room and draw whatever you wanted." It gave him a chance to explore and play with some of his ideas. But, he adds, "After a period of time it felt like I was locked in the room."

Before Burton left Disney, he made a second film, *Frankenweenie* (1984), which was intended to accompany a re-release of Disney's classic *Pinocchio* (1940). *Frankenweenie* is about a little boy whose dog is hit by a car and killed. The boy revives the dog, Frankenstein-style. Like *Vincent*, *Frankenweenie* was designed by Burton's friend Rick Heinrichs, who has worked as a visual consultant on all of Burton's movies except *Batman*. Filmed in black-and-white, this live-action short is both wonderfully funny and oddly disturbing—something that can be said of most, if not all, of Burton's subsequent films.

Burton's vision may be unusual, but it is the opposite of chilling. When, for example, Jack wanders alone in despair through the forest (below), he seems all too human.

"When Disney saw *Frankenweenie*," Burton laughs, "they freaked out. The company was at a real transitional stage, and everybody was more afraid than usual. That's when I left."

A wide grin spreads across Burton's face. "So now," he says, "over ten years later, *Frankenweenie* gets released on video and *Nightmare Before Christmas*—which the studio originally rejected—gets made."

From *Vincent* and *Pee-wee's Big Adventure*, through *Edward Scissorhands* and *Batman*, to *Nightmare Before Christmas*, the leading characters in Burton's films are outsiders, misfits who live in worlds of their own. "There are things about me you can never know," Pee-wee Herman tells his would-be girlfriend Dottie. "Things you wouldn't understand. Things you couldn't understand. Things you shouldn't understand. I'm a loner, Dottie. A rebel."

Some of Burton's characters, like Pee-wee, are happy in the bizarre

Whether he is marveling at a snowflake in Christmas Town (opposite) or trying to get at the essence of a candy cane while conducting experiments in his tower (left), Jack Skellington has a boyish charm—"a lot of passion and energy," as Burton puts it. Burton's many drawings of Jack (such as the one below) capture this quality.

little worlds they inhabit. Others, like *Nightmare*'s Jack Skellington, are consumed with a longing for something different, something better. Edward Scissorhands longs to embrace the girl he loves, but can never do so because of the razor-sharp shears at the ends of his arms. Bruce Wayne is driven by his own dark obsessions to dress in a bat suit and roam the forbidding streets of Gotham City, doling out vigilante justice. Even though Burton's characters may temporarily attach themselves to a greater community, in the end they have only themselves.

Burton indicates that he is saddened by "society's tendency to categorize everyone." In part that's why he loves movie monsters like King Kong, Frankenstein's creation, the Creature from the Black Lagoon. "I feel for these characters," he confesses. "They're not bad; people are torturing them, attacking them."

Jack Skellington is Burton's way of reversing the movie monster stereotype. "He has a lot of passion and energy," Burton claims. "He's always looking for something. That's why I love him; he's looking for a feeling."

Burton emphasizes that "everyone has two sides to them." He believes, "it's a real struggle to go through life and figure things out—determining which is the dark side and which is the light." This attitude comes out in his characters. "There's something about my characters that goes against the grain of what the culture walks you into. It's not something I think about. It's not something that I go after. It's something that I can't help but feel."

HENRY SELICK

Although the very title of the film—*Tim Burton's Nightmare Before Christmas*—proclaims Burton's contribution, Selick, as its director, remains a key creative voice. "Tim Burton gave us a great story, great characters, a mood, a look, and we were able to turn it into a film," Selick says.

"I think Burton's influence is obvious," states supervising animator Eric Leighton. "But there's a lot more of Henry Selick's vision in this movie. To me, it looks more similar to some of the films I've worked on with Henry than to *Batman*."

In the eyes of co-producer Kathleen Gavin, *Nightmare* is decidedly a joint effort. She points out that even though this was a very special project for Burton, he entrusted it to another artist. That in itself is a strong tribute to Selick's abilities.

Selick's name is already familiar to many stop-motion connoisseurs. *Nightmare* is only the latest in a long line of beautiful, sometimes surreal, sometimes downright peculiar, films that he has directed. Most notable is a strange and intriguing short called *Slow Bob in the Lower Dimensions* (1990). Included in the Twenty-third International Tournee of Animation, this film was a major step forward creatively for Selick.

Selick explains, "I worked much more hands-on on all my films before *Slow Bob*. They were short films (*Seepage*, with life-size stop-motion

Burton and Selick (shown together, left and right respectively, in the photo opposite) were in constant communication, working well together. Although Burton was involved at every stage, Selick was at the studio every day overseeing work on the film: approving sketches (like the one for a Halloween toy opposite, far left), checking finished puppets (like the Mayor, below), and—most important—closely directing the animation in all the shots (as in the one at left of Lock, Shock, and Barrel staring with terror when Jack reappears after they thought he was dead).

figures; *Phases,* on animal metamorphosis exercise) and pieces for MTV (*Haircut M, Mask M, Xerox M,* etc.), on which I would write, produce, direct, storyboard, edit, build sets and puppets, and often animate, design, light, and make the coffee. On *Slow Bob* I took a big step up in the art of delegating."

Slow Bob is, in a way, a direct ancestor of *Nightmare Before Christmas.* They share an eerie beauty, an eccentric point of view, and a high level of technical excellence. This isn't surprising since, as Selick notes, "The core group that did *Slow Bob* is the group that's doing this movie." Supervising animator Eric Leighton, set supervisor Bo Henry, director of photography Pete Kozachik, editor Stan Webb, mold-making supervisor John Reed, animators Trey Thomas and Owen Klatte, and model makers Bill Boes and Merrick Cheney worked on both films.

Selick recalls his first impression of *Nightmare,* when Burton was developing the idea at the Disney Studios. "It was one of the most interesting projects I'd ever seen," he says. "Tim drew a sequence of Jack Skellington walking in the forest, discovering the secret doors to the holiday worlds, and Rick Heinrichs designed some sculptures of Jack and his dog Zero, which were just beautiful. So the beginnings of the film were planted in my mind over ten years ago."

In 1990 Selick was approached by Heinrichs and told that, after a decade in cold storage, *Nightmare* was going to be produced. According to Burton, Selick was "the only person I could think of who could pull this thing together. He is an artist, a wonderful animator."

Directing a stop-motion animated film is very different from directing a live-action movie. For one thing, the stop-motion director never gets to yell, "Action" or "Cut." For another, the stop-motion director doesn't work directly with the actors—only with the artists who make the actors act.

In the initial months of production, Selick spent his days going over the script with the story department, translating the script into storyboards, and discussing with various artists every aspect of the film's drama and design. "Very often," he says, "I'd have people do fifty or a hundred drawings of a sequence. Then I'd go back, rework it, pull shots, shift them around. When I agreed on the sequence we'd shoot the drawings on film and edit those. Then we'd redraw and rework the sequence and start all over again."

At the same time the characters were being designed, and the sets, props, color, and lighting were being developed. Selick's job involved making the rounds to each department, making decisions on even the most minute detail. Throughout, Selick constantly referred to Burton's original drawings, which influenced any new characters being designed.

He also worked closely with Heinrichs on the visual design of the film.

As design turned into production, Selick's job got far more complex. Every morning he screened "dailies" (the previous day's output), working with animators on a frame-by-frame examination of the completed shots. "There were so many camera stages going at this point," he explains, "that I would spend the entire morning looking at shots and working on various stages of shot development."

In the afternoons Selick initiated discussions of new shots, going over every facet with the animators, as well as the camera, light, and prop people. He also made the rounds of every department, offering suggestions, making decisions, giving orders, asking questions.

"My days were packed," Selick reflects. "The main thing is, I had my fingers on everything, but not constantly. My supervisors were so good that they could carry the ball for a long time. But it was important that I was at dailies every day, approving or influencing every shot."

The result of Selick's hard work is a brilliant, one-of-a-kind film that catapults the art of stop-motion animation to a new level. As Selick puts it, "This is by far the most ambitious stop-motion animated film ever done. It has the best budget, the highest caliber of talent, and it's by far the most artistically beautiful and interesting. This isn't just puppets; it's a whole world. After five minutes the audience will believe in that world, in the relationships and the story we're telling."

Selick's sense of fun allowed him to enter into the puppets' world (opposite). His input contributed to every drawing of a scene, such as this rendering of Santa's first view of Halloween Town when Jack opens up the sack.

 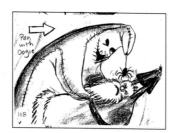  

I'm the Oogie Boogie Man.

  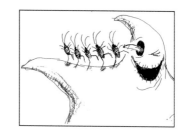 

Well if I'm feelin' antsy · and I've nothin' much to do · I might just cook a special batch

 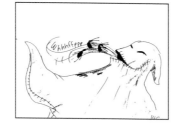  

of snake and spider stew.

OOGIE BOOGIE
And don't ya know the one thing that   (16A)

With his songs, Danny Elfman (opposite) brought many of the characters to life. This was especially true of Oogie Boogie. Working with the lyrics, the storyboard artists came up with the panels above—but then it was decided that creating tiny bugs with armatures allowing them to dance was asking for too much, so the sequence was altered. The lyrics, however, stayed the same.

DANNY ELFMAN

From the opening notes of his first orchestral film score—*Pee-wee's Big Adventure* (1985)—it was clear that Danny Elfman was the freshest, most interesting and eccentric film composer to come along in a great while. Elfman's quirky Nino Rota-esque music was the perfect accompaniment to the skewed vision of Tim Burton and Paul ("Pee-wee") Reubens, and he was immediately catapulted into the first rank of contemporary film composers.

Elfman has continued to provide highly memorable scores for Tim Burton's films, composing music that is clever (*Beetlejuice*), powerful (*Batman*), and achingly beautiful (*Edward Scissorhands*). He hasn't just worked with Burton, however; Elfman has composed dramatic, sometimes ironic, music for Warren Beatty's *Dick Tracy* (1990), John Amiel's *Sommersby* (1992), Sam Raimi's *Darkman* (1990), and Martin Brest's *Midnight Run* (1988), as well as working with directors like Clive Barker and Richard Donner. He has also made his distinctive voice heard on television, providing themes for the Fox animated series *The Simpsons* and HBO's horror anthology *Tales from the Crypt.*

But Elfman's contribution to *Nightmare Before Christmas* extends far beyond the musical score. Not only did he compose the music, he also wrote the lyrics—and he provides the singing voice for the lead character, Jack Skellington.

Elfman's involvement began simply enough. "Tim usually tells me about his next film while we're working on the film before," he recollects. "When we were working on *Edward Scissorhands* he told me about *Nightmare.* I was very enthusiastic."

"We actually worked on the music before there was a script," Burton says. He and Elfman began meeting at Elfman's home to talk the project over. "I'd say, 'This is the emotion in this part of the story,'" Burton recalls. "It was fun; we'd never worked that way before."

At the time, only the original poem existed, so their collaboration fleshed out the story. And as the story grew, so did Elfman's enthusiasm for the project. In fact Elfman was surprised at how quickly it all began to come together. "I've never worked that fast," he reflects, "but it was very simple and very clear. Tim and I know each other pretty well, so there was no reason to ooververbalize or overanalyze."

The ten songs that resulted from Elfman and Burton's meetings form the backbone of the film; they help define characters and advance the plot. Elfman took his lyrical cue from Burton's poem, sharing Burton's affinity for a "Seussian" type of rhyme. He even took a few of Burton's lines of dialogue and used them in his songs.

"Burton had a lot of images that I really liked," Elfman notes. "For example, he came up with the line, 'Perhaps it's the head that I found in the lake.' I thought, 'Oh, that's wonderful.' So I used it in 'The Town Meeting Song.'"

Upon completing each song, Elfman recorded it in his home studio, mocking up orchestration with keyboards and synthesizers, and singing it himself. "I sang all the voices on the demos," Elfman remembers, "except Sally's (it's in falsetto, so it would have been quite ludicrous). Tim and I stayed up all night in the studio, with me in the singing booth and Tim acting the part of record producer. It was great fun, and we were occasionally prone to fits of hysteria. As I layered all the voices— up to twenty for the Halloween chorus—Tim gave me wild hand gestures indicating his approval or disapproval. It was wonderfully insane."

Jack's fascination with Christmas Town is conveyed in several of his songs. Although he never actually enters Santa's house (shown in a color study at right), when we see it, we can almost hear Jack marvel, "What's This?"

One character, Oogie Boogie, came to life as a result of Burton and Elfman's memories of the cartoons they watched as children. "Danny and I both loved those old Betty Boop cartoons, where this weird Cab Calloway number comes out of nowhere, for no reason," Burton says. "I remember being young and watching these things coming out of nowhere; it was like I was hallucinating: 'Whoa! What's that?'"

While doing the initial recording of the songs, Elfman realized how attached he was to the songs he had composed for Jack Skellington. "Jack sings most of what he feels," explains Elfman. "All of his emotional transitions are in the context of the songs." In writing the songs, Elfman had, in a sense, brought Jack to life. The more he thought about it, the more he became convinced he could sing them best: "I strongly related to Jack's character, and I've been through many of the same emotional beats."

After starting his musical career in the off-kilter pop group Oingo Boingo, Elfman finds it a little amusing—and amazing—that he has now written and performed in a full-blown Hollywood musical. "We have really turned the clock back," Elfman chuckles. "This is more like an old-fashioned musical than anything done in the last forty years."

Elfman compares the development of *Nightmare* to the way Gilbert and Sullivan or Rodgers and Hammerstein may have worked years ago. But for *Nightmare,* unlike most musicals written by songwriting teams, Elfman was both the lyricist and composer. "It was just Tim and I," he explains, "and that made everything very clear and simple."

CAROLINE THOMPSON

Nightmare Before Christmas marks the second time that Tim Burton has worked with screenwriter Caroline Thompson. From the beginning, the two seemed to be kindred spirits. "When I worked with Caroline on *Edward Scissorhands*," Burton says, "we got along really well. She understands me. She's able to tap into a certain emotional quality that's very important for the kinds of films I do. On a film like *Nightmare Before Christmas* it would be very easy to overwhelm an audience with technique. But Caroline understands the medium and how to get at the emotional quality that the film needs."

Thompson didn't start out in the film business. Born and raised in Washington, D.C., she published her first novel, *First Born,* when she was twenty-six. Her agent introduced Thompson to Burton while he was filming *Beetlejuice.* He read and admired *First Born,* and soon after the two began to collaborate on the bittersweet fantasy *Edward Scissorhands.*

"Tim had this brilliant image," Thompson recalls, but he hadn't fleshed out the story. "The minute he said to me, 'It's about this guy who's got scissors for hands'—bang! I knew the story. His image was so resonant and so powerful, it was such a clear expression of feelings, that the whole thing took off. The story is about not being able to touch anything, about feeling that everything you touch turns to tatters. It's about being awkward. In doing the script for *Edward Scissorhands,* I got to write about childhood for me and, I think, for Tim also."

Thompson didn't start out writing the screenplay for *Nightmare Before Christmas.* But it soon became apparent that a fresh vision was needed, so Burton asked her to join the team. Ironically, Thompson was already involved in the project—although not exactly directly.

As Danny Elfman explains, "Caroline and I were living together at that time, so that she was forced to listen to the songs day and night as I was composing them. I think that it may have been driving her a little crazy in fact. And

Caroline Thompson (above) fleshed out the story with her script, giving Halloween Town (in a drawing below) a more three-dimensional feeling by creating various goings-on around Jack.

One of Thompson's most important contributions was to give Sally a believable personality with some spunk. Although at times Sally (like Jack) bemoans her fate (right), she takes action to get what she wants and do what she thinks is right. Thompson also helped develop characters like the Mayor, who travels around Halloween Town in his executive hearse (shown in a prop design opposite, bottom).

by the time she got involved, she was more than a little aware of the project, as she knew every song by heart."

"Clearly, when we needed someone to come in and pull it all together," Elfman continues, "Caroline was the natural choice. She was already indoctrinated into the project. She actually heard every song before Tim did, because I tried them out on her. 'Let me just run this by you,' I'd call out as she climbed up the stairs."

Elfman's songs told the basic story, forming the core of the film. But there were still gaps in between, where the story needed to be filled in. "It was a strange objective," Thompson comments. "I had to write a story to thread Danny's songs together, to fill out characters who weren't fully formed."

Elfman and Burton were busy fleshing out the songs, and Henry Selick and an initial crew of artists at Skellington Productions in San Francisco were already hard at work creating preliminary storyboards and designing characters, sets, and props. When Thompson officially signed on as *Nightmare*'s screenwriter, she found herself in the slightly uncomfortable position of attempting to impose a structure on a film that was already going nearly full steam. "I felt like I had to design the house after everybody was living in it," she says.

As a first step, Thompson went away and wrote a complete script. But that was far from the end. She then sent her script to Skellington Productions in San Francisco, where the storyboard artists reimagined her words in visual terms. They then faxed new images to Thompson, and she in turn incorporated their ideas into the script. Slowly, with much back and forth, the script evolved.

One of Thompson's tasks was to keep the story in focus. "I think a writer's most useful purpose on a movie," she underlines, "is to remind everyone, 'No, Sally is there on purpose. It wasn't an accident. This scene ties in with the next; don't forget.' The people making the film tend to be mono-focused, while the writer is able to step back and see it as a whole."

In Hollywood, once a film is in production, the writer is frequently the one member of the crew who is left out of the creative process. Producers and directors usually feel no hesitation about rewriting the script on a whim. Thompson has seen that side of the business and believes that her experience on *Nightmare Before Christmas* was unusual in this regard. "They were enormously respectful of my different opinions," she indicates. "Although I sometimes had to say, 'Don't forget to count me in,' that was less true on this project than on any other."

Thompson is convinced that *"Tim Burton's Nightmare Before Christmas* is a very, very special film. It's an amazing technical accomplishment, which is a delight for adults. At the same time it's very much a children's film—always was."

KATHLEEN GAVIN

Keeping in close touch with producer Denise Di Novi, Kathleen Gavin, the co-producer, oversaw the day-to-day activities of Skellington Productions. Working out of her spacious office in the San Francisco studio, Gavin faced challenges and problems of a unique nature. She refers to Skellington Productions as a "kind of a guerrilla production company," adding: "We were set up specifically to do this project; no feature film had ever been made this way before. The building was empty, and we had to start from scratch, figuring it out as we went along."

Because of the demands of such a large-scale stop-motion production, people didn't play the traditional roles they would have played on a normal feature. Everybody had to be flexible. As co-producer, Gavin found her job was "to keep it all going on a daily basis: get the director what he needed, make sure we were staying on budget and schedule, and all those kinds of things. My long-term job was to figure out how we would get to the end, in terms of support for the picture. At one point we had to build more stages so the question became: What kind of scheduling problems does that create? And the big question was always: How do we clone the director?"

Gavin is a Disney veteran. Before working on *Nightmare,* she acted as associate producer on *The Rescuers Down Under* (1990) and production manager on *Oliver and Company* (1988). For her, the first shock in moving from conventional cel animation to the three-dimensional world of stop-motion was the prodigious amount of preplanning that was necessary for every frame.

"In cel animation you can draw anything," Gavin explains. "But on *Nightmare* there were very real limits in terms of the sets we could build. A layout in cel animation can be used for one scene, then another. You can pass it on to the next person or photocopy it, so they can both work on it at the same time. Here, we had to build duplicate sets, duplicate puppets; it was a very different world."

Because no stop-motion feature had ever been created on such an elaborate scale, Gavin and production manager Phil Lofaro were put to the test in anticipating the production's needs. "We didn't have any blueprints to follow," she says. "Should an animator animate twenty-five frames a day or eighty frames? If you're doing cel animation, you can check on previous pictures to see what was done. That was never the case on this project."

One result of this "learn as you go" approach was that the production kept growing and schedules had to be rearranged. *Nightmare* was continually evolving. "When we started, there wasn't a completed script," Gavin points out. "Ideally, you want to complete the storyboards, then have it all on a story reel before you even start production. Of course, that never happens—and it certainly didn't happen in this case. We started boarding in July 1991 and started production in October, and we didn't really finish the reel until the next May."

As the project grew, so did the staff. On an average week Skellington Productions employed a crew of between ninety and one hundred people. More hands were added when a particularly large set was being constructed or extra sculpting had to be done. And, of course, the numbers decreased as departments finished their work. About midway through the production, there were eight animators working full-time on thirteen or fourteen different stages around the studio. But within a few weeks, the number of animators grew to twelve working on nineteen stages. Even then, all the animators together produced only about seventy seconds of finished film per week.

According to Gavin, "Animators were our scarcest resource. It's very hard to find animators who can do work at this level." Special effects and animation studios were scoured in San Francisco and Los Angeles, Chicago and London. Advertisements were run in papers throughout the United States, as well as in Canada and Europe.

For Gavin, the work on *Nightmare Before Christmas* lasted more than two years. In addition to the myriad of logistical problems that were her daily lot, she was faced with a trying but necessary discipline. She had to look at *Nightmare's* scenes repeatedly, day after day, month after month, without getting thoroughly tired of the whole thing.

"Sometimes you figure that you've seen this gag forty-seven times," she reflects. "I remember the first time I did an animated movie. I was sitting there after six months or a year, watching a scene again, and I thought, 'I remember laughing at this. I remember getting hysterical at this scene.' I've learned that I just have to keep in mind that I did laugh—that, yes, it works. It's very difficult, but you have to hold onto what you felt the first time you saw it; you really have to try to retain that."

What Gavin didn't have to fight to retain was the sense of excitement that came from helping to create something new and unique. "I've never done anything quite like this before," she says. "I guess nobody has. It's incredibly hard work, but the collaborative effort makes it extremely rewarding."

Kathleen Gavin (opposite, top) had to deal with the nuts and bolts of making sure everything moved along smoothly. With Selick and others, she looked at each day's footage, reviewing scenes like the one below (where Lock gets ready for Oogie's "show" with Santa) many times.

Denise Di Novi (above) helped to keep the whole project on track. She probably could sympathize with the Mayor in the shot below, right, when he can't find Jack (who's been gone all night) and he has to go ahead with the plans for the next Halloween.

DENISE DI NOVI

If producer Denise Di Novi works well with Tim Burton, it may be because they share a taste for the offbeat. *Tim Burton's Nightmare Before Christmas* is the third film on which the two have collaborated. As head of Tim Burton Productions from 1989 to 1992, Di Novi produced both *Edward Scissorhands* and *Batman Returns*.

Even the non-Burton films that Di Novi has produced are, to put it mildly, a little strange. She oversaw the sinister black comedy *Heathers* (1989), all about murder and popularity in high school, and the decidedly peculiar *Meet the Applegates* (1991), which concerns a family of Brazilian beetles in human form who live in an American suburb.

Perhaps because of their track record of making hits out of the unlikeliest of material, Di Novi says, she and Burton found little resistance from Walt Disney Pictures when they approached the studio with *Nightmare Before Christmas*.

Although the offbeat technique of *Nightmare Before Christmas* might have seemed like a hard sell, Di Novi claims the studio looked at the project as "the best Christmas present they had received in a long time! The drawings and the story were so compelling and the first tests were so beautiful that Disney was only excited by the project. I think that they were also pretty confident that whatever Tim does turns out to be pretty amazing."

Throughout the process, Di Novi indicates, "Disney was very in-

volved, but they were very respectful of our independence. It was a really good working experience. [Disney chairman] Jeff Katzenberg is a very smart man. He knows when you have a director like Tim, who has a vision, you don't tamper with it."

Getting approval from Disney, it turned out, was the easiest part of the process. The hard part was figuring out how to make this feature-length stop-motion animated film. Di Novi explains, "From a producer's standpoint, the challenge was to put together a good team, when most of them had done nothing like this before. Kathleen Gavin, who's fantastic, had never done stop-motion before, and many of the artists had worked only in cel animation."

According to Di Novi, the team had to undergo a "learning curve," figuring out, from the ground up, how to budget and schedule the production, because stop-motion animation had never been done at *Nightmare*'s level before. "Every week we had a lesson from the week before," says Di Novi, "and it took about a year to get an idea: 'Oh, this is how it's going to work!'"

Her first foray into producing an animated feature has left Di Novi impressed—and a little bewildered—at the meticulous, sometimes torturous process involved in giving life to inanimate objects. "To me," she says, "it's almost like a Zen discipline. It's so difficult to have that focus and concentration on such minute detail; everything's incredibly arduous. I thought that making live-action features was a slow, painful, painstaking process, but this is maybe a thousand times more so. It's amazing to me."

Zero's grave is really his home. The design was based on one of Burton's early concepts. The drawing below was done later from Rick Heinrichs's model of the Halloweenland cemetery.

FILM CREDITS
(credits not final)

Producers
Tim Burton
Denise Di Novi

Director
Henry Selick

Co-producer
Kathleen Gavin

Music, Lyrics, and Score
Danny Elfman

Screenplay
Caroline Thompson

Talent
Jack Skellington: Chris Sarandon
Jack Skellington (singing voice): Danny Elfman
Sally: Catherine O'Hara
Oogie Boogie: Ken Page
Mayor: Glenn Shadix
Evil Scientist: William Hickey
Lock: Paul Reubens
Shock: Catherine O'Hara
Barrel: Danny Elfman

Animation
Supervising Animator: Eric Leighton
Animators: Mike Belzer, Paul Berry, Kim Blanchette, Steve Buckley, Joel Fletcher, Angie Glocka, Tim Hittle, Owen Klatte, Justin Kohn, Loyd Price, Anthony Scott, Trey Thomas, Harry Walton, Richard Zimmerman

Camera
Director of Photography: Peter Kozachik
Camera Operators: Jim Aupperle, Jo Carson, Selwyn Eddy III, Ray Gilberti, Dave Hanks, Rich Lehmann, Pat Sweeney, Eric Swenson
Camera Assistants: Michael Bienstock, Mark Kohr, Sara Mast, James Matlosz, Carl Miller, Cameron Noble, Chris Peterson, Brian Van't Hul, Matt White
Rigging: Michael Johnson, George Wong

As is to be expected in working many hours under intimate circumstances, romances flourished among the crew members. The most fruitful was between Eric Leighton and Jill Ruzicka, resulting in nuptials and a beautiful bouncing baby boy named Oliver Thomas (below).

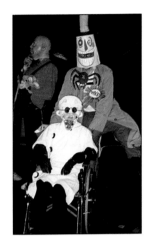
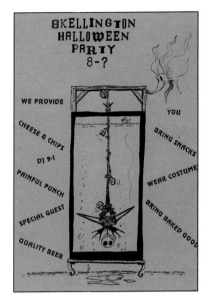

Art Department

    Art Director: Deane Taylor

    Assistant Art Directors: Kelly Asbury, Bill Boes, Kendal Cronkhite

    Visual Consultant: Rick Heinrichs

    Additional Character Designs: Mike Cachuela, David Cutler,

    Barry Jackson, Jorgen Klubien, Joseph Ranft, Christopher Ure

Story

    Storyboard Supervisor: Joseph Ranft

    Storyboard Artists: Mike Cachuela, Jorgen Klubien, Robert

    Pauley, Steve Moore

Character

    Armature

    Armature Supervisor: Thomas St. Amand

    Armature Engineers: Blair Clark, Merrick Cheney, Chris Rand,

    Lionel Orozco, Eben Stromquist, Bart Trickel

    Fabrication

    Character Fabrication Supervisor: Bonita DeCarlo

    Character Fabricators: Jeff Brewer, David Chong, Glenn

    Clifford,Chrystene Ells, Margot Hale, Liz Jennings, Barbara

    Kossy, Grace Murphy, T. Reid Norton, Facundo Rabaudi, Elise

    Robertson, Edytha Ryan, Valerie Sofranko-Banks, Lauren Vogt,

    Michael Wick

Mold

    Mold-Making Supervisor: John Reed

    Mold Makers:Jon Berg, Mike Grivett, Erik Jensen, Michael

    Jobe, Victoria Lewis, Tony Preciado, Rob Ronning, Willem

    Van Thillo

For a Halloween party, many people came dressed as characters in the movie. Jack, the Mayor, the Evil Scientist, and Oogie Boogie all appeared. There was also a snake charmer, who brought four huge snakes and draped them over willing partyers.

Sculpture

Character Sculptors: Shelley Daniels, Norm DeCarlo, Randal Dutra, Greg Dykstra

Set

Set Construction Supervisor: Bo Henry

Set Designer: Gregg Olsson

Set Foreman: Tom Proost

Set Builders: Phil Brotherton, Phil Cusick, Fon Davis, Rebecca House, Todd Lookinland, Ben Nichols, Alessandro Palladini

Set Technicians: J. D. Durst, Aaron Kohr

Lead Backgrounds Painter: B. J. Fredrickson

Set Painters: Jennifer Clinard, Loren Hillman, Peggy Hrastar, Linda Overbey

Model Shop

Model Shop Supervisor: Mitch Romanauski

Prop/Model Makers: Nick Bogle, Joel Friesch, Pam Kibbee, Paula Lucchesi, Jerome Ranft, Marc Ribaud

Set Dresser: Gretchen Scharfenberg

Fx Animation

Effects Animators: Gordon Baker, Scott Bonnenfant, Chris Green, Nathan Stanton

Cel Painter: Loretta Asbury

Editorial

Editor: Stan Webb

Assistant Editor: Edie Ichioka

Apprentice Editors: Andrea Biklian, Patti Tauscher

Track Reader: Dan Mason

Music Editor: Bob Badami

Production

    Production Manager: Phil Lofaro

    Auditor: Kevin Reher

    Production Coordinators: Jill Kuzicka, George Young

    Artistic Coordinator: Allison Abbate

    Stage Coordinator: Alia Agha

    Stage Manager: Robert Anderson

    Assistant to Producer/Director: Gisela Hermeling

    Assistant Auditor: Jenny Spamer

    Assistant Production Coordinator: Kat Miller

    Assistant Artistic Coordinator: Shane Francis

    Production Assistants: Susan Alegria, Jon Angle, Thomas
Buchanan, David Burke, Daniel Campbell, Anne Etheridge,
David Janssen, Denise Rottina, Beth Schneider, Kirk Scott,
Arianne Sutner, David Teller

ACKNOWLEDGMENTS

The writing of this book has been at precisely the opposite pace of the creation of *Tim Burton's Nightmare Before Christmas.* Where the art of stop-motion animation is almost unbelievably methodical, precise and slow, my job has been accomplished in a frenzy. Happily, everyone concerned with this project has been helpful and friendly. Writing this book has been a little like riding a rocket into space; it took my breath away, but I wouldn't have missed the experience for anything.

First, I want to thank my collaborator Elizabeth Annas, a brilliant photographer and my treasured pal. Michael Singer's generosity and friendship can in no way be repaid by a simple acknowledgment here. Thanks, Michael, and remember the Alamo.

Many thanks to the nice folks at Tim Burton Productions: Diane Minter, Jesyca Durchin, Wendy Breck, and Jill Jacobs. For sharing their knowledge, talents, and time with me, thanks to the gifted artists at Skellington Productions, especially Kelly Asbury, Gordon Baker, Mike Belzer, Paul Berry, Bill Boes, Mike Cachuela, Blair Clark, Kendal Cronkhite, Bonita DeCarlo, Norm DeCarlo, B. J. Fredrickson, Kathleen Gavin, Angie Glocka, Bo Henry, Gisela Hermeling, Owen Klatte, Pete Kozachik, Eric Leighton, Dan Mason, Gregg Olsson, Joe Ranft, John Reed, Mitch Romanauski, Anthony Scott, Henry Selick, Deane Taylor, and Stan Webb.

Stacey Berman-Woodward and Scott Tobis transcribed some of the interviews, earning the mantle of Hero. Amy Toomin pointed me in their direction, for which I owe her a hot dog at Papoo's. Lee Tsiantis provided me with crucial videotape, pulling me out of the fire yet again.

Tim Burton, Denise Di Novi, Danny Elfman, Jeffrey Katzenberg, and Caroline Thompson took time to talk with me when they had better things to do. I thank them all for their highly informative and enjoyable conversation. I especially thank Danny Elfman for the use of his lyrics.

Thanks to Bob Miller and Mary Ann Naples of Hyperion for their guidance, to Susan Meyer and Sue Heinemann of Roundtable Press for editing and pulling all the elements of the book together, to Sylvain Michaelis and Joe Bartos of Michaelis/Carpelis Design for their beautiful design, to Beth Braunstein of the Walt Disney Company for help with stills, and to the staff of the Margaret Herrick Library of the Academy of Motion Picture Arts and Sciences for assistance. I don't see how a film book can be written without the aid of the Herrick Library.

Thanks to Pete and Molly for appearing just when I needed a shot of adrenaline. There's a squeaky copy of "The Daily Growl" in this for you.

And—finally—thanks to the best agent in the free world, Kay McCauley, and my great friend Thomas W. Holland, for their endless support and encouragement.

PHOTO CREDITS

The following credits are for photographs only (not artwork). Abbreviations are: t (top), m (middle), b (bottom), l (left), r (right).

Photos by principal photographer Elizabeth J. Annas: 32bl; 93; 98; 101; 102 (all); 114 (all); 115bl; 116tl, ml, mr; 118 (all); 119br; 120tr, ml, mr; 121tl, mr; 122 (all); 124–25 (all); 126br; 127–31 (all); 133bl; 134–36 (all); 138–41 (all); 142tl, tr; 144tr, ml, br; 148tl, br; 149l; 150–51 (all); 153, 154bl, br; 157tl, bl; 161; 162tl; 168; 172; 174; 177; 179; 182, 186.

Still photos by Bo Henry and the camera crew: 10, 12–14, 17, 25, 27, 30, 32br, 33, 36, 37, 40, 41, 43–45, 50, 54, 56, 57, 59, 63, 64, 65, 67tr, 69, 71, 72, 75, 78, 86, 88, 90, 104br, 105, 119t, 121tr, 152, 154t, 164–65, 169–71, 173t, 180, 183, 184b.

Additional photos by: Phil Bray (115br; 120b; 137ml; 144tl; 148tr, ml; 157tr, mr; 159), © Richard Downing (189), © Joel Fletcher (2–3), © Sue Heinemann (67bl; 116tr, b; 117br; 119ml), ©Bo Henry (123), © James Matlosz (142b, 147, 149r, 155), © Jenny Spamer (187 [all]), © Zade Rosenthal (184tl), and © Eric Swenson (16, 145–46 [all], 156).

INDEX